Tales From Toadsuck, Texas

Bill Cannon

Republic of Texas Press
Plano, Texas

Library of Congress Cataloging-in-Publication Data

Cannon, Bill.
  Tales from Toadsuck, Texas / Bill Cannon.
      p. cm.
  ISBN 1-55622-799-X (pbk.)
  1. Collinsville (Tex.)—History—Anecdotes.   2. Collinsville (Tex.)—
  Social life and customs—Anecdotes.   3. Country life—Texas—Collinsville
  —Anecdotes.   4. Collinsville (Tex.)—Fiction.   5. Country life—Texas
  —Collinsville—Fiction. I. Title.

  F394.C6945 C36 2000
  976.4'557—dc21   00-045889
                                                            CIP

Republic of Texas Press is an imprint of Wordware Publishing, Inc.
No part of this book may be reproduced in any form or by
any means without permission in writing from
Wordware Publishing, Inc.

Printed in the United States of America

ISBN 1-55622-799-X
10 9 8 7 6 5 4 3 2 1
0011

All inquiries for volume purchases of this book should be addressed to
Wordware Publishing, Inc., at 2320 Los Rios Boulevard, Plano, Texas 75074.
Telephone inquiries may be made by calling:

(972) 423-0090

Dedication

This book is lovingly dedicated to my late brother-in-law, Jim C. Graham. Jim was born in Collinsville, Texas, which was originally called Toadsuck. Had Jim lived during the days of Toadsuck, with his personality and business acumen, I am sure he would have been president of the Toadsuck Chamber of Commerce.

Author

Contents

Contents

Contents

Contents

Acknowledgement

I have numerous persons and organizations to whom I am indebted for making this book possible. The person I am most indebted to must remain anonymous, as her name has slipped from my grasp. While recovering from a total hip replacement in a Dallas, Texas hospital, the subject of my writing about Texas came up while having lunch with other patients. One lady, who was rather old and whose name I never knew, asked me if I had ever written about Toadsuck, Texas. After the laughter had subsided, I admitted that I had not, but that if there ever was such a place in Texas, the very name warranted further research and perhaps even exposure in print. She told me it was in Grayson County.

I appreciate her sharing this unusual bit of Texas history with me and the response from all whom I told about Toadsuck evoked such laughter, I was inspired to not only expose the town in writing, but to build around it a collection of fictional stories about the folks whom I imagined might have lived in a town bearing this name. The result is *Tales From Toadsuck, Texas*.

I would like to acknowledge the valuable assistance in researching the original Toad Suck, Arkansas, provided me by the United States Corps of Engineers Little Rock District in Little Rock Arkansas, Col. Thomas Holden Jr. Commander.

I am grateful to Mr. Tom Scott of the Faulkner County Arkansas Library, who happens to be a native of Toad Suck, Arkansas for his valuable assistance in my research of the original Toad Suck.

I must acknowledge the assistance of the Sherman Public Library for sending me material from the History of Grayson County, Texas, which was of immense value in my research.

As usual, I acknowledge the *Handbook of Texas* for providing information not only on the Texas town of Toadsuck, but on its native son, former Oklahoma governor, William, (Alfalfa Bill) Murray.

As usual, the reference librarians in the Dallas Public Library, particularly Heather Williams and Tina provided copies of vintage newspapers needed to be accurate in describing events in Toadsuck's colorful history.

Much information about early Collinsville, nee Toadsuck, was obtained from Mr. O. M. Quattlebaum and Mr. Noel Lewter. They were invaluable in my research.

I am grateful to Xina Davisson of the Whitesboro *News Record* for her research of old Collinsville newspapers. Ginger Garvin of the Whitesboro library assisted me in locating copies of vintage Collinsville newspapers.

I especially appreciate the assistance of my friends Bob Neff and Fred Buenrostro, who acted as readers of my tales and helped me decide which ones were "keepers."

To each and all of the above, I say thanks for helping me produce this humor book.

B. C.

"Yes, Virginia, There is a Toadsuck"

Toadsuck Texas, like Bug Tussle in Fannin County, is one of those Texas towns that falls into the "You're pulling my leg" category. But, like Bug Tussle, Toadsuck does exist! Originally called Toadsuck Saloon, according to the Grayson County Genealogical Society, the town later became a part of Collinsville in western Grayson County. Settlers arrived in the area in the late 1850s. In 1869 a town site was surveyed near the Toadsuck Saloon. The town of Toadsuck took the name of the saloon. It may have been named by early settler John Jones, after the city of Toad Suck, Arkansas

We spoke with Tom Scott at the Faulkner County Arkansas Library. Tom, who hails from nearby Toad Suck provided us with an abundance of information about Texas's Toadsuck's Arkansas namesake. We are grateful to this real-life Toadsucker for his assistance in confirming there really was a Toad Suck.

In Arkansas they divide the two words. A brochure published by the United States Corps of Engineers of the Little Rock District shows the original Toad Suck, Arkansas ferry as being where SH 60 crosses the Arkansas River. The brochure tells us, "Legend has it that long ago, steamboats traveled the Arkansas River when the water was the right depth. When it wasn't, the captains and their crews tied up to wait where Toad Suck Ferry, Lock, and Dam span the river. While they waited they refreshed themselves at the tavern there, to the dismay of the folks living nearby, who said, 'They suck on the bottle 'til they swell up like toads.' Hence Toad Suck. The ferry is long gone, but the legend remains."

The development of Texas's Toadsuck, while less earthy, was economically sound. Historical records show that the Texas and Pacific Railroad lines were built within three-quarters of a mile of Toadsuck in 1880. By 1897 most of its businesses and residents had moved to the tracks. The railroad town was named Collinsville. Toadsuck produced future Oklahoma governor, William Henry (Alfalfa Bill) Murray. Although its twenty-eight-year existence is, by Texas standards, short, its residents left a legacy of humorous stories that bordered on philosophy.

We have interviewed former patrons of Opal's Kurl Up and Dye Beauty Salon, and the Toadsuck Domino Parlor and faithfully recorded the stories they remember floating around the community during its peak period. It was a bit like eavesdropping on the community's party-line telephone, or reading back issues of Toadsuck's weekly paper. The stories reveal a little about the folks of rural North Texas when life was less complicated.

Toad-Facts, an Introduction to Toadsuck

While this collection of humorous stories about the folks I imagine might have lived in a town burdened with a comical name like Toadsuck is fictional, there are some interesting true stories associated with this small Grayson County, Texas town that were sometimes as humorous as the fictional ones. We have chosen to begin this book with these historically true stories. In this way we can preserve some of the lore surrounding this town with a name that is sure to raise eyebrows and more than a little disbelief!

Toadsuck's Controversial Native Son

William Henry (Alfalfa Bill) Murray, whom we respectfully call controversial, would have been called simply "cantankerous" and "sot-in-his-ways" by folks in Toadsuck, which tells a lot about the inhabitants of this Grayson County community.

According to the *Handbook of Texas*, Murray was born November 21, 1869, in the village of Toadsuck near Collinsville, Texas. He obtained a teacher's certificate when he was nineteen years of age. Murray was twice an unsuccessful candidate for the Texas Senate. After passing the bar examination, Murray practiced law in Fort Worth. In 1898 Murray moved to Tishomingo, Indian Territory, then the capital of the Chickasaw Indian Nation. There he became active in the politics of the territory. He served as advisor to the governor of the Chickasaw Nation. He once actively advocated separate statehood for eastern Oklahoma.

Following his marriage to a part Indian woman, Murray moved to a farm where he grew alfalfa. His lectures to farm groups on behalf of this crop earned him the sobriquet "Alfalfa Bill." In 1930 Murray made a third and successful attempt at being elected governor of Oklahoma. Murray had the dubious distinction of attracting national attention because of his eccentricities and his dramatic use of executive powers.

Perhaps his best-known example of being at loggerheads with society occurred in July of 1931 when he defied a court order to open a free bridge across the Red River. Murray had used his executive power, which he held "superseded" federal law, to call out the National Guard to block use of the offending bridge. This resulted in what became known as "The Red River War."

Red River War

The Red River Bridge controversy, sometimes referred to as "The Red River War," which pitted the governor and citizens of Texas against the governor and residents of Oklahoma, occurred in July of 1931, over the opening of a free bridge built jointly by both states between Denison, Texas, and Durant, Oklahoma.

The Red River Bridge Company, a private firm, which operated an already established toll bridge that paralleled the free bridge, attempted to prevent the opening of the new free bridge. The company claimed that the Highway Commission had earlier agreed to purchase the toll bridge for $60,000. A temporary injunction was issued and Texas governor Ross Sterling ordered barricades erected across the approaches to the new bridge. Oklahoma governor Murray opened the bridge by executive order, claiming Oklahoma's half of the bridge ran north and south across the Red River, which Oklahoma had title to as a result of the Louisiana Purchase Treaty of 1803. Texas Governor Sterling ordered a detachment of three Texas Rangers, accompanied by Adjutant General William Sterling, to rebuild the barricades torn down on orders of the Oklahoma governor. The Oklahoma governor ordered Oklahoma highway crews to tear up the northern approaches to the still operating toll bridge and ordered traffic over the bridge to halt. Mass meetings were held in Denison and Sherman demanding opening of the free bridge. In special session the Texas legislature passed a bill granting the Red River Bridge Company permission to sue the state of Texas to recover the sum they claimed was owed them.

On July 25 the free bridge was opened to traffic and the rangers were withdrawn. In a federal court in Oklahoma, Governor Murray was enjoined from blocking the northern entrance to the toll bridge. The Oklahoma governor still had a card or two to play in this bridge war! The governor declared martial law in a narrow strip along the northern approaches to both bridges. He argued that, as commander of the Oklahoma National Guard, he was above the federal act. Murray ordered the National Guard to the bridge and, according to some published reports, he showed up at the bridges with an antique revolver, "making a personal appearance at the war zone," as some newspapers branded it!

The Burial of Toadsuck's Not So Favorite Son

The Feb. 21, 1932 edition of *The New York Times,* reporting on Oklahoma governor "Alfalfa Bill" Murray's bid for the Democrat party's nomination for the U.S. presidency, gave the following account of his return to the place of his birth to launch a publicity drive for his campaign. Under a headline reading, "HE JOURNEYS TO TOADSUCK" the reporter writes "Town of his birth has changed its name, but love for famous son remains." Of the candidate's February 18, 1932 return to Toadsuck the reporter writes, "Murray launched his greatest publicity drive this week when he trekked to Durant near the Red River on Wednesday where a great mob of Murray-for-president patriots assembled to join their hero on a trip to Toadsuck in Grayson

County, Texas, on Thursday. You will not find Toadsuck, Texas on the map. It has gone highbrow since that bleak day sixty-two years ago when Bill Murray was born at the sprawling crossroads. Today the town is known as Collinsville. There a monument to Murray, Toadsuck's foremost son, was unveiled." The reporter goes on to add that "There was a crowd of thousands at Collinsville. Murray looked upon his triumphal cavalcade to Collinsville, or Toadsuck, as he prefers to remember it, as good national publicity."

If local historians' memories of the "triumphal cavalcade" are correct, the reporter's editorial comment to the effect that "the town's love for their famous son remains," was highly inaccurate! Old-time Collinsville residents remember Murray Day, as the event was called, differently. The former mayor of Collinsville recalls that a life-size statue of the former governor was, indeed, to have been dedicated by "Alfalfa Bill" upon his arrival from Oklahoma City by train. The townsfolk were excited about the big celebration, as "Governor Murray Day" had generated much enthusiasm in the small town. Local residents expected to make some money from the highly publicized visit. Some were charging for parking cars on their property, and many stands selling various items had been erected. Barbecuing of calves and goats assured the availability of food for the onlookers.

The former Collinsville mayor remembers that Murray had to be coaxed to the rear platform to address the throng of citizens gathered to see and hear the guest of honor. It didn't take but a few words of slurred speech to determine why the honored guest couldn't be easily coaxed from the train. His drunken condition resulted in a very brief stay in Collinsville by the guest of honor.

The hasty retreat of Toadsuck's native son brought "Bill Murray Day" to an early close. The conduct of the would-be nominee for president of the U.S. so infuriated the residents of Collinsville that his statue was later pulled down by a team of horses. The statue was broken apart when it was pulled down and is buried under the parking lot of the Collinsville State Bank.

The New York Times gave no account of the presidential candidate's conduct that so unceremoniously kicked off his national publicity campaign.

These turn-on-the-century buildings, built around 1900, were once the heart of downtown Collinsville, after the rout of the KATY Railroad brought about the demise of Toadsuck and created Collinsville. This area was once called Silk Stocking Street.

Burial site of Oklahoma Governor "Alfalfa Bill" Murray's statue, which was pulled down by citizens disappointed by the governor's brief stay during Murray Day, Feb. 18, 1932. The statue was buried under the bank parking lot, which is now a storage lot behind Lewter's Cabinet Shop. Although consideration has been given to unearthing the statue, no one is exactly sure where it is buried.

Once the Adamson Hotel and stage stop, this residence originally stood in Toadsuck. It was later the home of Hattie Light. The Grayson County History says that this building was the birthplace of Will Adamson, longtime Dallas educator and namesake of Dallas' Adamson High School.

Barlow Feeney's Comeuppance

Toadsuck's resident practical joker Barlow Feeney, known for existing solely off the practical jokes he pulled on anyone who was innocent of the man's reputation or gullible enough to fall into one of his usually costly and always embarrassing practical jokes, got his comeuppance in spades during the fall deer hunt this past year.

Barlow had begged to be included in the Toadsuck Domino Parlor's annual fall deer hunt. The three regulars on the deer hunt put their heads together and finally agreed to include the joker with the understanding that the gasoline and food expenses would be split four ways, with each man paying the tab every fourth stop. They fully hoped that Barlow's coming would reduce the total expenses for all.

What they hadn't counted on, although they should have, was that Barlow's bag of practical jokes was far from empty. Barlow was sitting in the back seat of Gilbert Dinsmore's '62 Pontiac sedan when they pulled into the first service station to fill up. Barlow volunteered to pay for the first fill-up. When the tank was full, he rolled down the car window and tendered the attendant a hundred-dollar bill. Now bills of this size were scarce in and around Toadsuck, and the wide-eyed attendant apologized and said he couldn't change the big bill. This forced one of the men in the front seat to have to pay the tab. Barlow feigned embarrassment and said he would take care of lunch.

The lunchtime tab was again paid by Barlow with his one hundred dollar bill. The small greasy spoon restaurant could not change the big bill, and once again one of the men in the front seat was stuck with the food bill.

Barlow's one hundred dollar bill got extensive use during the trip to and from the men's annual deer hunt. By the time they neared Toadsuck on the return trip, the regular hunters' expenses were higher than any other previous hunting trip. But the victims in the front seat didn't take Barlow Feeney's little "big bill" attempt at avoiding paying his share lightly! Their combined efforts to give Barlow an expensive lesson in the Golden Rule proved to be both expensive and "golden." Expensive for Barlow and golden for the other hunters who would spend many hours gleefully describing how Barlow got his just comeuppance that fateful hunting trip.

Thadd Bristow from Bristow's Hardware tells it best. "We were nearly home with Barlow into us for about sixty dollars when Clif Pearson opened his 'lessons learned in a barbershop' book. We were about out of gas and when we pulled into the Gulf station at Dixon Gap, Clif got out of the car on the pretense of using the men's room. Once inside he cornered the youthful attendant and told him he would be offered a hundred-dollar bill in payment. Clif told the young man it would be worth his while if he would accept the bill, saying he could change it. When the tank was full, Barlow, as was expected, rolled down his window and tendered his well-worn hundred-dollar bill. Once the attendant had a firm grip on the bill, Clif sped away, leaving a young attendant looking at the first hundred-dollar bill he had ever seen. The shouts of protest from the man in the back seat fell on deaf ears! Barlow's hunting trip, which usually costs each participant about sixty dollars, cost the new member of the hunting party a full one hundred dollars."

This was the last time Barlow Feeney begged to be included in the Domino Parlor's men's deer hunt.

A Fading Life of the Party

It's no wonder that Ophelia Hawthorne's kids gave her a cruise to the Caribbean for her eightieth birthday. "Miss Ophelia," as she was called, had always been at the forefront of Toadsuck's social whirl, such as it was. She was the first to arrive at anyone's private soiree, or at any of Toadsuck's publicized events that even smacked remotely like a party. Even as she grew older, "Miss Ophelia" was anything but a party pooper, outlasting most of those in attendance at most gatherings.

Not addicted to strong drink, Ophelia could imbibe with the best of them who were, and still remain charming. The only time anyone could remember Ophelia missing out on any of Toadsuck's social events where alcohol was in evidence was the brief period of time in 1930 when she was recuperating from a cracked rib suffered when she fell from a barstool at the Eastern Star officer's installation. The two months Ophelia took as a hiatus from Toadsuck's social whirl only served to build up a Sahara-like thirst for John Barleycorn. This is why local townsfolk were not surprised at Ophelia's asking for a cruise for her eightieth birthday. She had seen too many ads touting the abundance of bar accommodations on most cruise lines. Once aboard, according to Ophelia's son-in-law, Clifton Spivey, Ophelia wasted no time making it known what she was celebrating! At the ship's main deck bar she announced loudly that she wanted a drink in celebration of her eightieth birthday. The bartender asked what she wanted. "I want a scotch and two drops of water," she replied.

After she finished her drink, a young man sitting nearby said "I want to buy the lady a drink for her birthday." Again she ordered a scotch and two drops of water. The ship's purser, who overheard that the passenger was celebrating her eightieth birthday, insisted on buying her a drink to help her celebrate. "And," he asked her, "what are you drinking?" "I'll have a scotch and two drops of water."

After sitting the drink in front of Ophelia, the bartender said, "Miss Hawthorne, I am dying to ask, out of curiosity, why is it that when you order your scotch, you only want two drops of water?"

"Well, young man, if you must know, at eighty years of age, I can still hold my liquor, it's my water that gives me a problem."

Who Said Homework Wasn't Important?

Ten-year-old "Pink" Crowder hadn't yet lived long enough to learn the most famous of all "no-nos" involving women. One day he approached his mother, Ollie Mae, who worked at Opal's Kurl Up and Dye Beauty Salon on Hackberry Street just off the square in Toadsuck. Perhaps she was just tired from standing on her feet and fiddling with all them old ladies' hair, he thought. Otherwise, why would she get her panties in a wad over such a simple question as "How old are you?"

Pink really didn't know exactly how old his own mother was, it was plain as that. How better to find out than ask her outright, he thought. But her tone of voice and the bulging veins in her forehead, which were usually reserved for those nights when Pink's daddy had showed up about an hour before supper time and announced that he had invited a couple of visiting men from his home office for dinner. Even Pink, at his tender age, could understand why a woman, picky as they were, would get a burr under her saddle over such unthoughtful conduct. But one's age is a matter of unchangeable fact. However, the boy learned, in no uncertain terms, this was an unapproachable subject, period.

"Son," said Pink's mom, "there are two things a gentleman never asks a woman, her age and her weight!" With that explosive lesson in chivalry, Pink dropped the subject, temporarily.

"Then," asked the youngster, "will you tell me why you and Daddy got a divorce?"

"I will not!" she said. And there were those bulging veins again! "That is just too painful a subject, and you are too young to understand, anyway, just drop the subject and do your homework."

Pink dropped the matter, but the whole afternoon's dialog stayed in his head till next day at school. During his shower following Phys Ed., he called Eddie Dunlap, who was a couple of years older than he was, over to sit with him while he dressed. He felt Eddie must be wiser than he and perhaps might shed some light on the entire "women thing," as Pink called it. Sure enough the twelve-year-old provided him with a wealth of help. Although not a deep insight into the "women thing," it was to solve Pink's immediate curiosity about his mother's age, and a bit more! Eddie, obviously a more mature male, lived up to Pink's expectation.

"All you want to know about your mom is on her driver's license," whispered Toadsuck's twelve-year-old man of the world, as the boys huddled in deep conversation alone in the boy's gym locker room. "Some time when your mom is out of the house look in her purse for her license. There you'll find your answers."

Taking Eddie's advice, one Sunday when his mom went to Clemmie Barlow's baby shower next door, Pink, bent on finding out why his mom was so secretive about her age, carefully rummaged around until he found his mom's purse. He scanned the details of her driver's license as though he was a spy for some foreign country in possession of the nuclear missile sites map of the U.S. Department of Defense.

A few days later, after he was certain she had not detected the invasion of her privacy, he approached her. "Mom," he said smugly, "I know how old you are and how much you weigh. You are thirty-eight and weigh one hundred thirty-nine pounds." Feeling very sure of himself, he continued, "I even know why you and Daddy divorced."

"And," responded his shocked and curious mother, "why did we divorce?"

"Because you made an F in sex!" replied the very confident ten-year-old.

Primate in the Pulpit?

Those attending the 1938 protracted meeting at the Mulberry Street Baptist Church got more than they bargained for, as did Reverend Clifton Clowers of Tulsa, Oklahoma, who had been brought to Toadsuck by the congregation to hold its annual summer revival. The renowned evangelist had been known to conclude a week's meeting by baptizing six or eight new converts.

One thing that made the evangelist so popular was what he called his "traveling question box." The preacher always placed his question box at the back of the sanctuary and invited those attending his meeting to insert questions, which he tried to answer sometime during the meeting.

One night following a real "hell-fire and brimstone" sermon, Brother Clowers took a slip of paper from his coat pocket that had come from the question box. "The question is," announced Brother Clowers, "What is the difference between an ape and a Baptist preacher?" The peeved preacher flushed a little but was not to be flustered. He said, "I don't think I can answer this question without being biased, but if the person submitting the question will come up here and stand by me, I think the congregation can tell the difference!"

So, Sue the Stork!

Folks who think all babies are as cute as the one on the baby food jar never saw the offspring of Jasper and Oneida Calhoun. Their baby Leonard's jaundiced skin color and protruding ears made him look like a taxicab with the doors open. Even Leonard's mother said she was relieved when little Leonard needed changing. That way she could look at his other end for a few minutes! Oneida spent many tearful hours after listening to neighbors and friends make fun of her new baby. She was especially upset when a Toadsuck neighbor suggested she invite P.T. Barnum to her baby shower. They had the nerve to suggest that this might go a long way to insure a lasting career for the child. But nothing upset Oneida as much as what happened on the T&P train trip she made to Fort Worth to visit a friend who had moved there from Toadsuck to go to work for a major long haul trucking firm.

In those days the railroad had vendors, called "butcher boys," who walked through the cars offering candy, fruit, and other snacks for the comfort of the passengers. One such vendor heard the sobbing of a woman as he went from one car to the next. Upon investigation, he discovered Oneida with her baby cradled in her arms. The passenger was bawling her eyes out. The "butcher boy," in an attempt to represent the railroad in a positive manner, asked the Toadsuck resident what the problem was.

"I'm just crushed," said Oneida. "I've never been so insulted in all my life. I'll never ride this railroad again! The conductor," she explained, "said my baby was the ugliest he had ever seen in all his years working for the railroad." Oneida could barely tell the young man her story because of her constant sobs.

The young man looked sympathetically at the passenger and, in an effort to dull the thoughtless conductor's remarks, said, "I apologize for the rudeness shown by our conductor, and I would like to do something to make amends in some way. Won't you accept this free banana for your monkey?"

More Dollars Than Sense

Nobody ever claimed that Feeney Poovey was the brainiest resident in Grayson County, and there are still a few folks around who can remember the day he proved it, when the original Toadsuck Saloon was still around. Popular as the aging watering hole was, Tuesday night was still a slow one for the establishment. Its most recent proprietor, Benny Boswell, decided it was time to do something to promote Tuesday night!

Having visited Fort Worth on a buying trip, Benny took a page from the big city boys' book and, not being able to promote a "Ladies' night out" for fear of bringing down the wrath of the W.C.T.U. (Women's Christian Temperance Union) on the saloon, he decided to try to circumvent the organization, which was influential in many Texas towns, by promoting a special offer not directed at attracting women customers. Benny brought the town out into the streets when he strung a brightly painted banner from the front of Toadsuck's famous saloon that read, "All you can drink for a dollar!"

Although not a candidate for an intelligence contest, Feeney could at least read. And he had never in his life read anything like what this eye-catching banner proclaimed. His boots left a cloud of dust as he beat a hasty trail into the saloon that gave the town its name. Those who sit around at the Toadsuck Domino Parlor swear that Feeney's blatant display of ignorance went this way:

Feeney elbowed his way through the crowd of men already crowded before the bar by the sign designed to attract everyone of drinking age in the county. He timidly asked the barkeep on duty if he had read correctly, that one could drink all he wanted for a dollar? The already swamped barkeep wiped his hands on his apron and confirmed to Feeney that he had read correctly. Feeney, his right hand stuck deep in his pants pocket, smiled and asked, "Then how much can I drink for two dollars?"

No Replacements Wanted!

Horace Bains' barn burned and his wife, Clara Lee, called the family's insurance agent to report the loss. "We had the barn insured for $50,000, and I would like to get a check right away."

"Whoa up a minute," replied the agent, "insurance doesn't work that way. We have to ascertain the value of what was insured and then provide you with a new one of comparable worth."

There was a long pause at the other end of the line, and then Clara Lee replied, "In that case, I'd like to cancel the policy on my husband."

Toadsuck's Golden Glove Award

Although not many folks in Toadsuck had time for the foolishness of sporting events, having to devote most waking hours to scratching a living from the land or what few jobs were available in the small town, with the advent of radio many of Toadsuck's menfolk became great fans of baseball, as they could listen to both the minor and major league games at night and on Sunday afternoon when they were free from their labors.

As a result of this addition to their meager culture, the Farmer's Co-Op Gin decided to form a baseball team to play other teams in Grayson County that had suddenly sprung up. Fortunately, Delbert Shockley, who taught mathematics and was the boys' Physical Education teacher at Toadsuck High School, knew the rules for baseball and had his own ball and bat. As a result, Delbert got the job of head coach and manager for the new team. At season's end the Toadsuck "Toads" had won more games than any other semi-pro team in Grayson County.

As promised by Barrow Bates, the Co-Op's president, the "Toads" were to be rewarded with a dinner at Dingle's Hot-Gut Barbecue Restaurant on State Highway 12, at which time each member would receive a trophy for his part in bringing the team through a successful season. Thinking it would be good for his gin business, Delbert decided to invite the winning team from the women's church softball league to join the men at this award ceremony. Delbert got absolutely no complaints from the members of his team about the ladies joining them for dinner. One member of the Holy "Smokes" from the First United Methodist Church at Dixie was the team's beautiful blonde pitcher, Tammy Jean Higgins. Tammy was seated across from the "Toad's" star first baseman, Leander Philpotts, who had made quite a name for himself for turning the double-play. "Hands" Philpotts, as he was known, was in for a reward beyond all expectation. By the end of this banquet of ribs and brisket he would have truly earned the Golden Glove award for the season.

Just after the first serving of ribs and prior to the coleslaw, the gorgeous blonde, whom Leander had been giving the once-over most of the evening, was the victim of a freak accident, which gave the timid Leander a chance to speak to her. Just as Tammy Jean leaned over to help herself to the coleslaw, she sneezed and her glass eye flew out toward Leander. The star first baseman responded reflexively and snatched her eye in mid-flight! "Oh my goodness!" gushed the blonde as she put the eye back in place. "I have ruined your evening! I must do something to make up for it. Let me take you out for dinner."

The couple met a few nights later at another Toadsuck eatery where they really had a pleasant meal, after which Tammy ordered drinks. After she paid for dinner and drinks, she invited Leander to her house for breakfast the next day. Leander, infatuated by his newfound friend, accepted. The next morning he was delighted by Tammy Jean's sumptuous full-course breakfast, including tomato juice cocktail, bacon and eggs, pancakes, and hot coffee. The first baseman was amazed at this treatment.

"I admired you from the first time you sat down across from me at Dingle's Hot Gut Barbecue Restaurant. You are an amazing woman. Are you always this nice to every guy you meet?" he asked.

"No," she replies, "You just caught my eye!"

Role Models

Just because you take your children to church every Sunday doesn't mean you are being a good role model for them. "Cotton" Browder thought his boy Billy was about as solid as any kid his age he had ever seen. Cotton credited the boy's behavior and demeanor to his being brought up going with the family to church each Sunday. "That kid knows how important church life is and has grown up expecting to be sitting in the Lord's house on Sunday morning."

On more than one occasion Cotton bragged about how he thought the folks in Toadsuck's First United Methodist Church had contributed greatly to Billy's heading in the right direction, although other boys his age teased him about being dragged to the church house for two boring hours each weekend, when he could be playing ball. "Yes," said Cotton "those church members have really made a great impression on Billy. We here in Toadsuck need more role models for our young people."

But the impression Billy was getting of the faithful brethren at the church was, in reality, somewhat different from what Billy's father thought. This was evident by what was reported by Miss Minnie Blalock, Billy's Sunday school teacher! She cornered Cotton in the church foyer when Sunday school was over and told him that if nothing else, Billy was paying attention in church. She said in class she asked him why folks should be quiet in church. Billy promptly answered where all could hear, "Because people are sleeping!"

Cold Hard Facts?

While Jeremiah Dunlop, one of Toadsuck's early settlers, might stretch the truth a little, we didn't believe he would downright lie about something. A few days ago, in a conversation with Benchly Crowder down at Clif Pearson's barbershop, Jeremiah told a story that might have stretched things so far they would snap back like a brand-new slingshot!

In a conversation about the morals of today's young people, Jeremiah insisted that Williard Tetlow, who used to have Tetlow's Furniture and Undertaking Parlor before he moved up North somewhere to take over a farm left to him by his great uncle, had a problem that was akin to the reprehensible conduct of many of today's youngsters. "And," said Jeremiah, "he solved it with a most drastic but successful move."

Willard, said Jeremiah, fell heir to a parrot when his widower uncle died, leaving him the bird, which had been his companion during his career in the U.S. Navy. Willard, according to Jeremiah, was quite fond of the talkative bird, which was an oddity in the small rural community of Toadsuck. His only complaint about the colorful bird was his embarrassing language. The bird's association with his previous owner's shipmates left him with a vocabulary of words that were not acceptable in mixed company. Every sentence he uttered was sprinkled with swear words of the foulest kind. As much as he was personally fond of the intriguing and somewhat interesting companion, he just could not tolerate his language. He had put Willard on the defensive on more than one occasion.

Having never had a bird as a pet, Willard was at a loss as to how to discipline the creature. He tried yelling at the parrot when he swore, but the parrot only squawked louder, using the vilest of language! Finally (and this is the part of Jeremiah's story that creates some question as to the truthfulness of his tale), Willard decided to take drastic measures to emphasize his displeasure with the bird's language. The next time the parrot exhibited his bad habit of using foul language, Willard opened the freezer of his refrigerator and threw the bird in without so much as a sweater! He left the parrot there for five minutes. After that time he heard not a squawk nor flutter of feathers from the bird.

Willard began to have pangs of regret over the severe punishment he had inflicted on the parrot. Jeremiah insisted that Willard told him with a straight face that he went to the freezer and opened the door. Out stepped the frosted but alive bird. The parrot then said to Willard, "I know my language has been an embarrassment to you and has caused you many sleepless nights, and for this I am sorry and beg your forgiveness. I will never use the bad language I learned from my shipmates, again. But," continued the contrite, colorful parrot, "I have one question."

"What is your question?" asked Willard.

The parrot fluffed up his red and green feathers and looked Willard in the eye and asked, "What did the poor chicken do?"

Sharing is Part of the Toadsuck Philosophy

One day during the noontime rush at the Toadsuck Diner, a very old couple walked slowly in. They gave the appearance of having been married long enough to have celebrated their golden wedding anniversary. They were a little out of place in what had become a favorite place to hang out for the younger folks of

Toadsuck. But the little old man walked boldly up to the cash register and placed his order.

They were watched intently by the much younger couples as their order was picked up by the little old man. On his tray were a single hamburger and one package of French fries accompanied by one cold drink. You could almost read the minds of the young couples who were watching so intently. "Look at those poor folks, they have probably lived together sixty years and can only afford one meal between them."

They watched as the little old couple took a seat. The old man then carefully unwrapped the hamburger, neatly cut it in half, and placed one half in front of his gray-headed wife. Then he counted the French fries, dividing them into two neat piles. He put one pile in front of his wife. The little old man took a sip from the drink that he had placed between them. His wife then took a sip and replaced the cup between the two. Once again he took a sip as he started to nibble on his half of the plain hamburger, and one could notice some of the other customers growing fidgety. Just as the old man started to eat from his pile of French fries, a young man stood and walked over to the old couple. He politely offered to buy another meal for the old-timers. The old man looked up long enough to say, "Thank you, but we are just fine. We are used to sharing everything."

The crowd noticed that while the little old man had nibbled away at his half of the hamburger, the old lady had not eaten a single bite. She just sat there watching her husband eat and occasionally taking a sip from the drink they shared. Once again the young man came over and begged the old couple to let him buy them a meal. This time it was the woman who spoke, "No, thank you, sir, but we are used to sharing everything."

As the little old man finished his half of the hamburger and was neatly wiping his face with a paper napkin, again the young man, who could stand it no longer, came over and repeated his offer to buy the couple another meal. After being refused for the third time, he asked the lady the question that plagued the minds of all the diners who had watched this shared meager meal. "Ma'am, why aren't you eating? You said that you shared everything. What are you are waiting for?"

The little old lady answered, "My turn with the teeth!"

City Folks Are So Sophisticated

Jo Edna Blevens was so pleased when her brother, Frank, who worked for the Texas Electric Railway System headquarters in Dallas, wrote inviting Jo Edna's nine-year-old daughter, Roberta, to spend part of the summer with him and his wife, Mary Pearline. Jo Edna thought the exposure to the more sophisticated atmosphere of the city, brief as it would be, would broaden Roberta's education far better than her schooling in Toadsuck. Now, Jo Edna reasoned, she could be exposed to new ideas associated with the hustle and bustle of urban living. How grateful she was to Frank and Mary Pearline for inviting the little Toadsuck girl into their home and their enlightening lives.

Roberta was not long in learning how knowledgeable her Uncle Frank was. Clutching her free interurban ticket in her sweaty little hands, she boarded the green and cream-colored railway car, which went like greased lightening from Denison to Dallas, where she would be met by her benefactor, Uncle Frank. The electric railway car whizzed through what, to Roberta, seemed like hundreds of little towns bearing the same characteristics as her hometown of Toadsuck.

As the electric railway car pulled into the Jackson Street terminal of Texas Electric in Dallas, Roberta broke into a broad smile seeing Uncle Frank, as planned, waiting for her. What was not planned, and what was to be her first "intellectually broadening" experience, was brought about by her arriving precisely at the same time as the railway car from Waco. She watched with childish curiosity as the Waco passengers departed their car. The first passenger to step from the Waco car was a colored woman about forty years of age. There being no people of color in Toadsuck, Roberta was shocked momentarily by the woman's skin color. She tugged at her Uncle Frank's hand, to which she clung with all her young grip. "Look, look, Uncle Frank," the little visitor from Toadsuck exclaimed. Once getting Uncle Frank's attention, Roberta gasped, "Uncle Frank, that woman has a black face...and," she continued all in one breath, "her arms and legs are black, too!"

Slightly embarrassed at the country girl's making such a fuss in public, Uncle Frank shushed Roberta as well as he could and, bending down to her level, quietly said, "Darling, the woman is black all over."

At this revelation, Roberta leaned over to her Uncle Frank and in awe said, "Uncle Frank, you know *everything*!"

An Enlightening Experience

The 2600 block of Mayhaw Drive in Toadsuck was not an ideal place for one given to strong drink to live. Bernie Solomon had built all of the little white frame shotgun houses on the street exactly alike. The string of rent houses were identical right down to the shrubbery in front of each house. This is why it was so illogical for Cyrus "Cy" Fenster, who was known to be one of Toadsuck's best-known town boozers, to move into one of the houses. There were times, it was said, when Cy was so soused, he couldn't hit the ground with his hat! "How," people asked, "could he find the right house after a night out on the town?" Several times, Cy told friends, he found himself waking up his neighbor after picking the wrong house. "Moving into this house was the best thing that ever happened to me," said Cy to a table of regulars at the Domino Parlor. He then went on to explain how the little shotgun house on Mayhaw Street saved his marriage and made a new man out of him.

"I came home late one night after a poker party at Hirum Peabody's garage, which included helping Hy dispose of a keg of home brew before his wife found out about his new brewing hobby. After waking three neighbors before I found the right house, I decided then and there it was time I devised a means of finding my house. I decided to put a red lantern on my porch when I went out, which would identify my house without a doubt.

"Sure enough on Saturday night, before meeting the guys from the job for our regular Saturday night poker party, I put a lighted red lantern on my porch. When I staggered home at two in the morning, there, like a lighthouse protecting the ships from going aground, was my beacon of mercy. The red lantern had saved me and my neighbors from another embarrassing meeting. So I picked up my homing light and walked to the door. I unlocked the door and made my way inside. Sure enough, I said to myself, this is my house. There is my favorite chair, with today's paper right where I left it. And there is my dining room.

"I then made my way to the back of the house. Yes, I said to myself, there is my bedroom with me and my wife in bed. Then, like a bolt of lightening sent from above, it hit me. Well, I thought to myself, if that's me and my wife in bed, who in the heck is this holding the lantern? And, boys, I haven't touched a drop of spirits since. That shotgun house turned my life around!"

Typically Texas

Rufe Garner loved Texas as much as anyone I ever met. While Toadsuck wasn't much to brag about, as Texans are prone to do, Rufe didn't let that stop him when he was around folks from outside the Lone Star State. It seems like Rufe was just a gifted liar to begin with. Not that all bragging about Texas was pure fabrication. Rufe just had a way about convincing an outsider that everything in Texas was bigger and better than anywhere else on the globe. It was like God had placed Rufe in Texas for the sole purpose of being its one-man Chamber of Commerce. And he was a good one, too! You just let an out of state car pause long enough at Toadsuck's one caution light, and Rufe would have the occupants willing to pull up stakes and move to Texas. They just shoulda kept their windows closed before Rufe could stick his head inside and start his sales pitch.

But Rufe was at his peak when he was able to visit other states, like on his annual vacation. This afforded the Texan a real opportunity, as everyone he met was fair game, all being "furriners," as Rufe called them. One trip to Louisiana, however, proved to be Rufe's undoing. He and Mary Pearline were visiting her parents' place when Rufe started his, "Everything is bigger in Texas" attack on the Louisianans.

While sitting on the front porch Rufe saw a jackrabbit cross the meadow in front of their house. "And," he asked, "just what is that?"

Rufe's father-in-law said, "That is a jackrabbit."

Rufe, unable to resist, said, "Back home our jackrabbits are so big, we hunt them with elephant guns." He had hardly got the words out of his mouth until a deer gracefully dashed across the field. Without waiting for any comments from his host, Rufe made it known that the animal was much smaller than Texas deer. "Back in Grayson County we don't even shoot deer that small because they would get overshadowed on the barbecue by the armadillos!"

About that time a big turtle slowly lumbered across the black-top that ran past the couple's house. "And," asked Rufe, "what is that?" It was then Rufe found out he'd met his match.

Rufe's daddy-in-law looked him in the eye and seriously said, "Better tuck your pants snugly in your boots, son, that is a Louisiana tick!"

"Let the Buyer Beware"

Jim Ed Biglow was one of those fellows who just had to learn things the hard way. It seems Jim Ed was always looking for ways to hold others responsible for his far-too-frequent errors in judgement. But his confrontation with Pastor Elihu Cranfield of Toadsuck's Bethel Baptist Church reached the height of audacity! What he did really emphasized the need to heed the Latin admonition "caveat emptor" (let the buyer beware).

It had been Pastor Cranfield's unfortunate "privilege" to unite Jim Ed and his bride of six months, Ruby Nadine Plover, in holy wedlock. It was obvious from the get-go to everyone but the love-blind Jim Ed that Ruby Nadine, although well beyond the flower of her youth, was not ready for the total commitment required to foster a full partnership marriage. An only child, Ruby Nadine was spoiled to having total attention lavished upon her, and Jim Ed's job as a milkman for Toadsuck Creamery resulted in his having, in Nadine's opinion, far too much contact with the womenfolk of the community.

The company's motto, "You can whip our cream, but you can't beat our service!" was taken to heart by many of Jim Ed's customers who didn't hesitate to phone Jim Ed at home to place their orders. Sometimes in "sickening sweet" whiny voices they apologized to Ruby Nadine for interrupting the privacy of Jim Ed's home life, then, for a quarter of an hour, instructed Ed in their dairy needs for the coming week. All this to the consternation of the new bride.

Jealousy might be too harsh an accusation to lay at the feet of the newly married Mrs. Biglow, but it was obvious to her milkman husband that Ruby Nadine would never abide Jim Ed's emptying any icebox drip pan other than hers! The big blow-up that brought about Jim Ed's confrontation with Pastor Cranfield grew out of Jim Ed's confession that Maudie Parker's leftover fried chicken, which he admitted sampling from her icebox, "was almost as good a day after it was cooked as Ruby Nadine's was the day it was cooked."

Ruby Nadine had thrown down the gauntlet. Either find a job that took him out of circles made of womenfolk or find someone else to cook his fried chicken. The "amen" to the Sunday closing prayer had hardly been said when Jim Ed walked straight to Pastor Elihu's office. "Pastor, do you believe in a man profiting from another man's mistakes?" Jim Ed asked.

"Why certainly not!" answered the surprised pastor.

"Then," replied Jim Ed, "would you please return the $25 I gave you for marrying me and Ruby Nadine last fall?"

East is East and Toadsuck is Toadsuck

Moon Mullins, who operated Toadsuck's largest construction company, was normally a very patient man. He had learned that dealing with construction workers required specific instructions, the simpler the better. Not because blue-collar workers were incapable of understanding, but because each had his own personal interpretation of what the boss meant when he gave instructions. It was difficult enough to get things done when dealing with the "good old boys" who grew up in and around Toadsuck.

But his ability to maintain his composure was bent to the breaking point the year that he hired Toadsuck's only Asian, Tommy Chan. The Chinese laborer was hired by Moon after he took up residence in Toadsuck when the T&P Railroad's bridge construction between Toadsuck and Greasewood was completed and Chan's services were no longer needed. He had been one of the last of the railroad's Chinese laborers brought from San Francisco when the tracks of the T&P were first laid in North Texas. Although he still displayed a definite Mandarin accent, up to now he had been a reliable worker. His assignment along with Yancy Darby and "Slats" Crowder proved to be his undoing!

Moon sent the three men to an almost completed construction site on the outskirts of the Dixie community. All the men had to do was move a large pile of gravel left over from the mixing of the concrete for the foundation of a new poultry processing plant scheduled to open the first of June. Moon met the three men at the site and explained that the owners of the plant were coming to inspect the progress of the construction and he wanted it nice and clean before their arrival. To make sure the three men knew exactly what they needed to do, he told Slats, "I want you to do the sweeping." He instructed Yancy to do the shoveling. "And," concluded Moon, "Chan, I want you to be in charge of the supplies." After making sure each man knew his assignment, Moon left to attend to other business.

As promised, Moon returned in about two hours to inspect the site, and to his chagrin, the gravel pile had not been touched. Moon was furious but managed to keep his temper in check. Calling Slats over he said, "Slats, why haven't you done the sweeping?" The longtime employee drew back in embarrassment and finally replied, "Mr. Mullins, I didn't have a broom and couldn't find the Chinaman to have him get me one." Moon then asked Yancy, "Why hasn't the gravel pile been shoveled up?" Yancy, without hesitation, said, "Mr. Mullins, I couldn't find a shovel, and the Chinaman who was in charge of supplies was nowhere to be found."

By now Moon Mullins was livid. His Chinaman in charge of supplies had let him down! He let his anger be known loudly and ended by saying, "I'm going to find that Chinaman and see why he hasn't provided the supplies."

About that time, the Chinaman leapt out from behind the gravel pile and with a broad smile, shouted gleefully, "SUP-PLIES!" This was the last time Moon Mullins ever hired a worker of a different culture.

Breakin' a Nasty Habit Aint Easy!

There was a time when most rural folks used tobacco in one form or another. Most men chewed plug tobacco. Brands like Red Man and white tag, thick plug Tinsley could be seen dripping from the corners of the mouths and ends of beards of many men who lived in Toadsuck. Women, on the other hand, dipped snuff, the most popular being Levi Garrett. Calhoun "Cal" Knowles, the community's postmaster, wouldn't be caught without a plug of Tinsley, no more than he would the galluses that held up his pants.

But use of the smokable, chewable plant was fraught with nasty practices, the most obvious of which was getting rid of the stuff. While both snuff dippers and tobacco chewers spit the amber juice into empty tomato cans, public places like hotels, saloons, and barbershops were expected to have highly polished brass spittoons sitting in strategic places to accommodate their customers. An accomplished tobacco chewer could make a spittoon ring like fine crystal with a good stout spit! Those of lesser breeding, on the other hand, left a trail of nasty brown stains on boardwalks and in some cases floors, much to the disgust of those in their company. Particularly the ladies whose dress hems were spattered by the uncontrolled tobacco juice.

A man's habit of random spitting seems to be a hard habit to break. Even when it is culturally unacceptable, the temptation to let one's juice fly at will must be overpowering. Or were Toadsuck's men just too "sot-in-their-ways" to accept newfangled ideas like spittoons? Even Cal Knowles, an educated, respected public servant, had an experience that is worth repeating.

One day when Cal went to Clif Pearson for his regular Saturday haircut, his jaw was puffed out like a kid's case of the mumps. He rolled his "chaw" around in his jaw all during the cutting of his hair. Although there was a shiny spittoon a couple of feet to the right of the chair, Cal's first deposit of the amber juice went on the floor almost directly in front of Cal. That is most probably where the postmaster had been spitting ever since he was man enough to cut off a chaw and give it a try.

Ol' Clif, meek as he is, said nothing and just took the toe of his shoe and nudged the polished receptacle in the exact spot where the customer spat. This evasive tactic didn't discourage Cal in the slightest. When he was about to choke from an over abundance of tobacco juice, he turned once again and sent a stream of juice onto Cal's floor. This time the patient barber made quite a show of using his foot to slide the spittoon into target range! Not a word passed between the two men, although Clif's inward rage was beginning to take the form of protruding blood vessels on his forehead and the length of his neck.

Things were brought to a climax the third time old Cal discolored the white linoleum covering the otherwise clean tonsorial parlor. When the barber nudged the spittoon in the direction of Cal's target area, Cal, to the surprise of the barber and a couple of waiting customers said, "Clif, I'm giving you fair warning; if you don't quit moving that damned thing in front of me, I'm going to spit in it!"

One of Clif's waiting customers howled with laughter, but Clif didn't even crack a smile. The only way you could tell he took notice of Cal's remark was that the blood vessel in his neck turned a purple color.

The Bare Facts in Rural Toadsuck

Toddie Lee Cowan was one of the few farmers who tried to make a go of farming when the town was passed by the railroad, resulting in so many folks moving away from Toadsuck. And if you want to know the truth, Toddie Lee really wasn't a farmer in the strictest sense of the word. Toddie Lee built several sheet iron sheds and went in the poultry business big time. He sold pullets to the processing plants in Denison and in Ardmore, Oklahoma. He also had a large egg business. The Cowans, to use a familiar expression, were "eating high on the hog," or chicken, depending on how you viewed the situation.

Their little business was situated out on FM 1562 on the way to Dixie. Toddie and Cora Lee found only one major drawback to their emerging "cackle-ranch." That drawback was man's attraction to the automobile and getting all the speed from it possible. Toddie Lee would often sit on the tractor he used to cultivate the maize he grew to feed to his poultry and lament about the increase of traffic on what used to be a quiet farm-to-market road.

It was not just the volume of traffic that troubled Toddie Lee, but the speed of the drivers, "In a hurry to the graveyard," as he put it.

Although most of the chickens were confined to the sheds, many were fenced in a large chicken pen surrounded by chicken wire from which some occasionally escaped. To house the entire flock, said Toddie Lee, would require the expense of erecting several more sheds at great cost. But as the traffic safety signs say, "SPEED KILLS." "You bet your boots," said Mr. Cowan, "speed kills my chickens!"

Toddie Lee called Sheriff Lynwood Timmons complaining about the speeding motorists killing a large number of his poultry population each month. "The bar ditches are littered with feathers from some of my best domineckers that have fell victim to conscience-less motorists who can't take their foot off the gas long enough to let my chicken make it to market."

"And," said the sympathetic but overworked sheriff, "just what do you want me to do about it?"

"I thought," said Toddie Lee, "you might come out here and put up some kind of sign that would cause motorists to at least slow down a little." Being an elected official, Sheriff Timmons said he would send the county to erect a sign. A few days later Toddie Lee saw the yellow county truck putting up a sign that read, "SLOW SCHOOL CROSSING."

A week passed and Toddie Lee was back on the phone to Lynwood Timmons. "Sheriff, that school sign, if it did anything, made the drivers go faster. Lost a half dozen of my best Rhode Island reds since the sign was erected!"

"Mighty sorry, Toddie Lee," said the solicitous officer. "I'll get another sign put up that should do the trick." Within a day or two a bright yellow and black sign appeared that said "CHILDREN

AT PLAY." This did no good. Toddie Lee thought motorists who were calloused enough to hit a poor, ignorant chicken wouldn't care if they hit someone's child at play! So, Toddie Lee was back on the phones almost daily for two weeks. "Well," said the sheriff, "I've done all I can."

"Is it okay if I put up my own sign?" asked Toddie Lee.

"Sure enough," said Sheriff Timmons. "Help yourself, and good luck." Of course Sheriff Timmons would agree to about anything to keep Toddie Lee off the phone. After about three weeks of silence from the poultry farmer, Sheriff Timmons decided to call and see how things were. "How is the traffic at your place, Toddie Lee, did you put up your own sign?"

"Sure did, sheriff, haven't lost a chicken since. Well, gotta go," said Toddie Lee. Better go and look at Toddie Lee's sign, thought the sheriff. If it's working for him, might be something we could use to slow speeders in town.

Sheriff Timmons went out to Toddie Lee's poultry farm and looked at the sign. It was a full 4x8-foot sheet of plywood lettered in yellow that read, "SLOW, NUDIST COLONY."

Scandal in Toadsuck

One would think that a community as small as Toadsuck would be less prone to scandal. That is perfectly true! In smaller towns, if it involves your family, it is called gossip. If it involves your neighbor, it is a scandal! That is exactly the case in the scandalous episode involving the town's longtime barber, Clifton Pearson. It was a well-known and frequent topic of conversation in Opal's Kurl Up and Dye Beauty Shop that Clif's attractive wife,

Bernice, was ten years his junior. Clif had operated his one-chair barbershop in Toadsuck as long as anyone could remember. As a matter of fact, Clif Pearson's revolving barber pole was the first electric sign in Toadsuck. No small thing to those who liked to brag about their local standing in the community!

This honor would not save the popular barber from the embarrassment he experienced as a result of the gossip caused by an event involving Douglas Timson, who operated Toadsucks's Five and Dime store. It all began one morning when Clif was just starting to work on his first head of hair of the day, and Doug Timson stuck his head in the door and breathlessly asked, "How long before you can take me?" Clif yelled, "About forty-five minutes." With that, Doug wheeled around and jumped in his '57 Chevy parked in front of the barbershop and sped off, leaving black marks on the pavement. He didn't come in all that day.

The next morning about nine-thirty, just after Clif opened, Doug, seeing one man waiting, popped in the door and asked. "How long before you can take me?"

"Got one waiting," replied Clif, "it'll be about an hour." With that Doug turned on his heels and jumped in his car and again sped away. While a bit puzzling to Clif, he didn't find it worth commenting on till the same thing happened again the third day in a row.

The afternoon of the third day, Clif got his shine boy, Willie, aside and confided to him his concern that Doug was going to another barber, perhaps in a neighboring town. Clif felt he was in no position to lose customers, even though his was Toadsuck's only barbershop. "I want you to be on your toes," he instructed his faithful shine boy, "and in the morning if Doug repeats his hasty retreat after finding out how long he must wait, I want you to follow him and see who he is going to for his haircut!"

Regular as clockwork, the next morning, as Clif was starting his first haircut, the proprietor of the dime store stuck his head in the door, as if on cue, and repeated his question as to how long he had to wait. When told an hour, he again made a hasty retreat to his car. This time the barber observed that he had left the motor running to assure a quick get-away. Clif gave the high sign to Willie, who was already reaching in his pants pocket for his car keys. Willie quickly put the final licks with his shine rag on the shoes of his first customer and headed for his car.

Clif thought Willie would never return with a report. But he had no way of knowing that the shine boy had to drive several miles out in the country. When he returned, Clif Pearson could hardly wait for the results of Willie's amateur detective work. "What did you find out?" he asked the shine boy.

"Why, Mistuh Clif," the young man stammered, "Mistuh Doug made a bee-line straight for your house!"

The Good Samaritan

Few in Toadsuck were better known or better liked for their simple good heartedness than Claude Ewell, who operated the Toadsuck Feed and Co-Op Gin. Claude had been known to pay top dollars per pound for the local farmer's cotton crops. It was a known fact that some farmers were given seed for next year's cotton crop at no cost. A deacon in the First Christian Church, Claude could be counted on to pitch in after a family tragedy such as fire, flood, or, as was the case in '36, tornado. But Mr. Ewell came mighty close last year to losing his religion altogether. It happened like this:

About four A.M. one cold winter morning Claude and Agnes, his wife of some thirty-odd years, had just gone back to bed after adding a couple of sticks of firewood to the big cast-iron pot-bellied stove that heated their bedroom. Both heard a faint tap-tap-tap on the front door. Neither responded to the faint noise, assuming it was a blowing shutter, instead. After a few minutes a louder knock was heard at the Ewell's front door. "Now, who could that be this early in the morning?" asked Agnes, who had just dozed off to sleep. "Dunno" said Claude, "guess there's only one way to find out."

With that, he threw back the toasty feather comforter that covered the pair and let his feet hit the cold hardwood floor. Must be pretty important to wake a person this time of night, he thought. "Only folks doing the milkin' are up and about at four A.M.," he muttered as he checked the time on the hall clock.

As he opened the heavy front door, he could see a man through the screen door standing on the gallery porch that surrounded the Ewell's big white frame house. "What can I do for you?" asked Claude in his usual friendly manner. The screen door permitted Claude to tell that the man reeked of alcohol. Perhaps to ward off the cold morning air, Claude opined to himself. Or was he being subjected to the lasting effects of a night out at The Red Rooster Roadhouse up on Highway 62?

"Can you give me a push?" asked the man with a slurred voice, the product of a tongue made thick by a night of serious drinking.

"No!" said Claude still upset by being awakened so early by the drunk.

"But, I really need a push," begged the drunk, whom Claude couldn't recognize in the dark of the early morning.

"Can't give you a push," insisted an irritated Claude. As Claude retreated from the front door in the direction of his still-warm bed, he was stopped by Agnes, who had been listening from the landing on the stairs.

"I'm surprised at you, Claude Ewell," said his wife in a no-nonsense voice. "You remember that snowy night we got stuck outside of Dixon when we were trying to get to Denison before Leon's baby was born? If it hadn't been for those nice folks who gave us a push, we wouldn't have seen our first grandbaby born."

Now, feeling fully chastised for forgetting his duty to his fellow man, Claude returned to the big front door. As he looked out in the still pitch dark night, he saw no sign of his early caller. Guess he gave up and left, he thought, but he couldn't have gotten but a few steps. "Hey you!" Claude hollered into the morning air. "You still need that push?"

"Yes sir, I do," came a reply from someone nearby.

"Well where are you?" asked a fully chilled Claude.

"Right over here in your porch swing, and I sure could use a push," came a slurred reply. Toadsuck's Good Samaritan turned and quickly made his way back to his bed, muttering a few choice words about the Golden Rule.

The Mule Egg

No matter how small, it seems like every Texas town has its resident con artist. Small as Toadsuck was, Barlow Feeney had already made his reputation throughout North Texas for his nefarious deeds. Barlow bragged about how gullible most folks were, especially those with the best education. Although some of Barlow's trickery could be costly for his victims, it wasn't the monetary gain that Barlow coveted. It was, as he admitted, the same thrill felt by a bass fisherman when he "set the hook" in the jaw of his prey. "And," he was quick to add, "to see the egg-on-the-face look on the victim's face when he finds himself suddenly the punch line of everyone's joke."

Barlow usually could be found sitting on a Dr Pepper case at Toadsuck's Fina station. It was there he had the best chance of finding uninitiated victims. Local folks knew Barlow well enough to question anything he proposed. At the Fina station, many out-of-towners paused to get information. If they paused long enough for Mr. Feeney to get his size twelve foot in their door, they were candidates for one of his scams.

You can see why Barlow's eyes brightened up that Saturday morning as the Mooney Motor Coach bus pulled in at the station, which Mooney used as a bus stop for that area. Barlow rubbed his greedy hands together, and a maniacal grin creased his face as a well-dressed man, who could easily have been a Yankee busi-nessman, strode up to Thedford Willis behind the counter and asked the distance to the Dixie community. Thedford told him it was about twenty miles due west. The man asked if there was a place where he could rent a buggy. Thedford asked the man if he could ride a horse, explaining there were no livery stables in Toadsuck. Getting an affirmative answer, he directed him to the

Toadsuck Feed and Implement Company. Thedford had unwittingly set the man up for what would be Barlow's pièce de résistance scam!

Barlow's con jobs were usually as uncomplicated as a simple shell game. His Academy Award con job became known in Toadsuck as "the Mule Egg caper." Barlow Feeney was leaning back in the shade next to the station's Coke box when he heard the man ask about the Dixie community. He also heard the visitor ask if there was a place he could rent a horse. Barlow's eyes lit up like Christmas in the Sears toy department. "A moment with you, sir," interrupted Barlow. "A horse at the feed store will cost you twenty dollars, and when you are finished with it, it will still belong to the store. And then Barlow "set the hook." "As a friendly gesture, I will gladly offer you one of my rare mule eggs for only ten dollars. Once the egg has hatched and you have used him for your trip to Dixie, the mule is yours to keep or sell at a nice profit. In order to reap the handsome profit, you must be willing to sit on the egg or otherwise keep it warm until it hatches."

The glow in the stranger's eyes betrayed his acceptance of Barlow's generous offer. "But," said the stranger, "I'll need some instructions. I don't know much about incubating eggs." As Thedford watched, Barlow reached into a burlap bag and produced a cantaloupe.

"Now," he said to his victim, "you just gently sit on this mule egg for two days, making sure it stays at body temperature, and in two days you'll have a fine Texas-bred mule. Just don't sit on the egg with full body weight, as it is much too fragile. I wouldn't want you to do anything to jeopardize your investment, small as it is," cautioned a somber-faced Barlow. "As long as you keep it tucked under you at all times, it will stay warm. In two days, you'll have a mule most any rancher would be proud to own."

The stranger reached into his vest pocket and produced a ten-dollar bill. "I want to thank you for not only saving me ten dollars on having to rent a horse, but providing a means of making some extra spending money. This must be what folks mean when they talk about Texas hospitality," gushed the proud owner of Barlow's rare mule egg.

The traveler walked away from the Fina station holding the cantaloupe close to his body to keep it warm. He decided he would spend the next two days in the Toadsuck Hotel, which would allow him to visit a friend there, as well as provide a place to sit on the valuable egg he had purchased. He carefully sat on the egg for one whole day and night. He was astute enough to know that he could not afford to have the egg hatch in his hotel room, so he decided to carry it on the road to his destination, Dixie, to sit on it the second day. Carefully, he positioned the egg so as not to crush its shell.

He spent the second night on a small hill overlooking a farmer's cornfield. He awoke the second morning after barely sleeping a wink due to the anticipation of the imminent hatching of the mule egg. As he eased off the egg that morning, the slope of the hill caused his precious egg to start rolling down the hill. The cantaloupe, which had become very ripe after two days of the victim's body heat, picked up speed as it bounced down the hill. It came to a stop when it hit a shock of corn stalks. The impact caused the melon to burst. It also startled a large Texas jackrabbit that was nesting in the corn stalk shock. The jackrabbit took off across the field in violent leaps and bounds. Right behind the jackrabbit at full speed sprinted the egg's owner, yelling, "Colt! Colt! Colt! Stop, here's your Mammy!"

Domestic Violence Toadsuck Style

It wasn't often that state trooper "Three Fingers" Findley drove off his usual stretch of Highway 82 to pay a visit to the Toadsuck area. So when his car's flashing red and blue lights were seen near the Dinwitty exit ramp, Riley Puckett from the Fina station couldn't resist making a dash down there to see what all the commotion was about. Trooper Findley, who got his nickname from an embarrassing shooting range accident, which cost him the first two fingers of his left hand, told Riley the entire saga.

The trooper said he stopped a man and his wife for speeding. "I told the driver he was doing seventy-five miles per hour."

"No," disputed the driver, "I was doing only sixty."

"You were doing about eighty," interrupted the man's wife. The man gave her a dirty look.

"And," added the officer, "I'm going to have to ticket you for having a broken tail light."

"Broken tail light?" asked the offender. "I didn't know my tail light was broken."

"Harry, you've known about that tail light for weeks!" said the wife.

The trooper continued, "I then informed the driver he would be given a citation for not wearing a seatbelt. The driver looked me square in the eyes and said, 'I took it off when you was walking up.'"

"Harry," interjected the wife, "you never wear your seatbelt."

The man turned to his wife and said, "For Pete's sake, can't you just shut up?!"

"I asked the woman if her husband talked to her that way all the time?"

"No," she said, "only when he's drunk!"

"Then," said the trooper as Riley stood there with a quizzical expression, "the husband threw a half-finished paper cup of Coke in his wife's face. I thought I ought to follow them home to make sure nothing more drastic would follow. Our job is to 'protect and serve' you know."

Riley just stood there transfixed by the story. "I didn't know for sure which one he was protecting," said Riley, as he finished telling the story to the awaiting crowd at the Fina station.

Taking a Bite Out of Crime

Miss Caroline Harris, the unmarried publisher of the weekly *Toadsuck Sentinel*, the community's local newspaper, and self-proclaimed town philosopher, published a story which, like so many articles appearing in her weekly, was of questionable origin. Mainly because if there was one thing Toadsuck didn't have, at least to my memory, it was crime!

Miss Harris reported that a burglar broke into a Toadsuck house one night. He shined his flashlight around the room looking for articles of value. According to Miss Harris' report, as he picked up a CD player to put into his sack, a disembodied voice echoed in the dark, saying, "Jesus is watching you!" He nearly jumped out of his skin. He clicked his flashlight off and froze in his tracks. Shaking his head, he vowed that after this job, he would give up his life of crime.

Just as he had regained his composure and started to disconnect the wires of a stereo set, clear as a bell he heard, "Jesus is watching you!" Totally rattled, he shined his flashlight frantically around the room. There in the corner of the room his beam of light came to rest on a beautiful red and green parrot. "Did you say that?" he snarled at the parrot.

"Yes I did," the parrot confessed. "I was just trying to warn you," squawked the bird.

"Just who do you think you are to warn me?" asked the burglar.

"Moses," replied the parrot.

"What kind of people would name a parrot Moses?" asked the intruder.

With hardly a pause, the parrot answered, "The same kind of people who would name a Rottweiler Jesus."

Like I said, Caroline's credibility is sometimes questioned.

The High Price of Honesty!

Hardly anyone in and around Toadsuck was surprised when Henry McClintok was hanged for murder. His escapades as a cattle rustler and highwayman in the early days of the county were common knowledge in Grayson County. The big surprise fostered by the event was the announcement in the *Toadsuck Sentinel* that Brother Lemuel Redmon, elder in the Toadsuck Church of Christ, was going to preach ol' Henry's funeral. Brother Redmon, who was one of the main teachers at the very conservative church, enjoyed a reputation for truth and honesty. Funerals, being what they were, usually overflowed with flowery words picturing the deceased as having one or both feet firmly planted on the streets of gold. Considering his criminal background and reputation as a scoundrel, folks couldn't help but wonder how Brother Redmon could preach ol' Henry through the pearly gates and keep a straight face.

The truth surrounding Brother Redmon's agreeing to officiate at Henry's "home going" service provides us with a real lesson in fancy religious footwork and the high price of honesty. Following ol' Henry's county-financed necktie party, Henry's brother Charlie went to several Toadsuck ministers asking them to preach his brother's funeral. But, because of Henry's well-known sins against the residents of the county, each refused on the grounds of bringing reproach against their respective churches.

In desperation, Charlie approached Elder Redmon, knowing how bad his little frame church needed operating expenses. Charlie offered the elder one thousand dollars to preach Henry's funeral. "Why," inquired Elder Redmon, "would you offer so much money for a service the church would normally render free?"

"Because," said Charlie, "there is a condition attached."

"And," asked Brother Redmon with a puzzled look on his face, "what is the condition?"

"I will give you the thousand dollars if you will call Henry a saint!" After thinking the proposition over, Elder Redmon agreed to the terms of the offer.

Those who attended Henry's funeral that day recall one of the most masterful pieces of oration they had ever heard. Elder Redmon gave the usual obituary information followed by the scriptural readings of "promise of eternal life" to those who were believers. In front of the rostrum, ol' Henry was laid out in his county-provided pine box and a black suit and tie. As he closed, Elder Redmon fulfilled the terms of his agreement. He lowered his eyes toward the deceased and, living up to his reputation for honesty, said, "Ol' Henry was truly a blight on Grayson County.

His sins are well known to most, but compared to his brother, ol'
Henry was a saint!"

Silence Can Be Golden

Next to Otis Campbell,
Feeney Dunlap was Toadsuck's
worst imbiber of alcohol.
Feeney was normally a harm-
less drunk. As a matter of fact
ol' Feeney could usually turn a
dull meeting of the Masonic
Lodge into a rip roaring time if
someone was thoughtful enough to
bring a pint of John Barleycorn with them. The biggest danger
from Feeney's overindulgence was when he decided he could
maneuver his car around the county, even though he couldn't hit
the ground with his hat! Pat Renfro, the Texas highway patrolman
assigned to District 26 of Grayson County, who was fondly called
"Officer Do-Right" by the residents of his district, which
included Toadsuck, regaled listeners with laughter when he
related his experience with Feeney the Monday after the VFW
annual javelina barbecue held just outside of Toadsuck at Vet-
eran's Memorial Park. As was to be expected, Ol' Feeney got a
snoot full at the picnic honoring the veterans of all wars. "It
seems," said Pat, "that Feeney got enough of the donated brew to
last him through the entire weekend. I seen him weaving from
side to side on FM 1226 and pulled him over. He smelled like a
busted vat at a San Antonio Brewery. Feeney asked me how I
knew he had been drinking. I told him, "When you made the

corner where Mulberry Street intersected the farm road, your wife was slung out of the car, and you didn't even slow down!"

"Thank God!" replied Feeney in a badly slurred voice. "I thought I had gone deaf!"

Family Secrets

Pastor Lester Dixon at the Toadsuck Full Gospel Tabernacle learned more than he wanted to at the Sunday morning service when he preached on "Perfection." After a well-studied lesson on the frailties of man versus God's expectation of Christians, he decided to put his flock to a little test to see how much they listened. Pastor Dixon asked the congregation, "Do you know any man who was perfect?" He glanced around the sanctuary to survey the hands that were held up.

Almost on his feet, at the rear of the congregation, waving his hand like a schoolboy who, for once, knew the right answer, was Elmer Dunlap, the owner of Dunlap's Five and Dime. When the pastor called on Elmer, the answer he got was not what he expected. "Elmer," acknowledged the pastor, "you know someone who was perfect?" When Elmer nodded in the affirmative, the pastor asked, "Who?"

"My wife's first husband," replied Elmer, as he shot a dagger-like glance at his wife, Bessie.

Farewell to House Calls?

The folks in Toadsuck and surrounding vicinity didn't take the news lightly. As a matter of fact most wouldn't believe it at all until they heard it straight from the doctor's own mouth. The town's first and only doctor, Ol' Doc Mckinzie, as he was fondly called, was retiring. This was announced first at the country doctor's church and then in a heart-warming tribute in the local weekly newspaper.

The publisher, everyone admitted, "outdid herself" in her flowery description of the service rendered by their beloved doctor over his forty-year tenure in and around Toadsuck. She brought out the fact that Ol' Doc Mckinzie's very first patient was a loud-mouthed customer at the now historic Toadsuck Saloon. Although long gone from the scene, there were still a few who remembered when the town's namesake was a well-patronized watering hole in North Texas. Now all that is a thing of the past, as was soon to be the case with Ol' Doc Mckinzie.

After the locals, many of whom the doctor had delivered, got over the shock of his retirement, the topic of conversation in every public gathering place was, "Who is going to take his place?" This was a legitimate question in those days, as doctors just didn't grow on trees! The departing doctor's patients expressed the community's concern and pleaded with their caregiver and close friend to put out feelers for someone to assume his practice who would be as skilled in medicine and bedside manner as he had been. This would not be an easy order to fill.

Realizing that it would take a lifetime of practice to learn the idiosyncrasies of each patient, which he knew was impossible, the retiring doctor had to use his judgement in selecting a replacement. One who would conduct himself in a manner that would enable the community to develop a trust in him. After a young doctor was decided upon and an exchange of letters resulted in the young physician's acceptance to move to Toadsuck and take over his practice, a meeting between the two doctors was arranged. It was in this meeting that the future of Toadsuck's medical care was determined.

Even before the retiring doctor reviewed his patients' case files with his replacement, the old doctor offered the replacement a word of advice not taught in medical school. "If these longtime patients, especially the aging ones, are to accept you, they must have total confidence that you know your medicine. Once the older ones respect your knowledge, they will bring any of the doubters around!"

"But," asked the new doctor, "how can I establish this trust that has taken you a lifetime of practice to build?"

"One thing you must never forget, if you forget everything else I say, is never change a diagnosis! If you change a diagnosis, the patient feels you are not sure of yourself. So stick with your first call."

The new doctor had barely got his shingle hung when he was visited by his first patient. Old lady Klendennen, whose previous file was inches thick, sat waiting for him bright and early on his first Monday morning in the old doctor's office. Her complaint was severe abdominal pain. After listening to her for her usual fifteen-minute review of her symptoms and a brief examination, he felt confident in making his first diagnosis in Toadsuck. "Mrs. Klendennen, he said, "you are suffering from locked bowels."

"Locked bowels?" she repeated, as a look of disbelief spread across her face. "How can that be? I've had diarrhea for a solid week."

Remembering the old doctor's stern warning about establishing trust and not changing a diagnosis, he smiled thinly and said, "That's what I mean, your bowels are locked wide open!"

Mrs. Klendennen gently squeezed his hand and said with a note of joy in her aging voice, "Thanks, Dr. Proctor, I'm so glad Dr. Mckinzie found someone so advanced in medicine, yet not so stuck up as those young doctors just out of medical school are."

The folks in and around Toadsuck had found a replacement for their old friend Dr. Mckinzie. "Now if this new doctor will just accept chickens and roastin' ears in payment for his services, things will be back to normal," they thought.

Better Safe Than Employed!

J. W. "Hickey" Brinkley was intrigued by the idea of becoming a state trooper. Mavis had been on him to get some kind of a job before the arrival of their new baby. When he saw in the *Toadsuck Sentinel* that applications were being taken for state trooper positions, he drove to Denison where the Department of Public Safety's North Texas headquarters were located. "Hickey" had hoped to be stationed in the Toadsuck area as he already knew who most of the lead-footed drivers were, which should, he thought, cut down on the amount of patrolling time.

Mavis was pleased that Hickey had been accepted into the trooper training academy and would start to work as soon as he passed his written examination following his training. The big day of his graduation from the training academy was a colorful event. Many of Hickey's Toadsuck cronies came to the ceremony just to see how he looked on the other side of a patrolman's ticket book!

This was never to be, unfortunately, as Mavis' husband flunked out during his examination. He was sailing along real good during the test, never once looking over at his neighbor's paper. Then it happened! The last section of the trooper's examination dealt with practical application of the trooper's training. Question number 100 was: "What would you do if you were on patrol and you saw a car containing two known killers following you at forty miles per hour?"

Without so much as a second's hesitation Hickey wrote, "fifty."

Toadsuck's Drug Problem

Folks today might be of the opinion that the country's much publicized drug problem is something to be laid at the feet of the latter part of the twentieth century. Not necessarily so! We folks who grew up in North Texas in the early part of this century have a vivid recollection of a shattering topic of conversation around the tables of the Toadsuck Domino Parlor. What was so shattering was that it involved dangerous drugs and one of Toadsuck's best educated, and highly respected professional men, Winton Gail Bodkin.

"Doc" Bodkin, as he was known by the folks in and around Toadsuck, opened Toadsuck's first drugstore while the town was still wet behind its corporate ears. Bodkin's was the place to go for all your pharmaceutical needs. Women talked just as freely with Doc Bodkin about their special problems as they did with the town physician. Doc Bodkin devoted one whole shelf to Cardui, "the woman's tonic," Midol, and other feminine remedies

related to "the woman's "curse."
With his knowledge of elixirs,
powders, and pills, it was a shock
that the much-discussed "drug
problem" ever happened. But
when you know the whole story,
the scenario seems more plausible. What makes it more plausible
is the second party in this small town drama.

Thedford Goforth worked at building a reputation as being the
town miser. The men whispered behind Thedford's back that the
otherwise likeable fellow "Wouldn't give fifty cents to see a
piss-ant eat a bale of hay!" When everyone chipped in to buy a
wreath for one of their forty-two partners at the Domino Parlor,
Thedford wouldn't contribute a dime, saying the deceased would-
n't know the difference if he did or didn't." That was just the way
old Thedford thought when it came to spending money.

One particular day Thedford had a blinding headache. It was
so bad that the miserly Mr. Goforth told the men at the Domino
Parlor he was going to Doc Bodkin's to buy, a term Thedford did-
n't use often, some aspirin. Doc greeted Thedford with a smile
when he walked in the drugstore. Getting a dime out of Thedford
Goforth made any of Toadsuck's merchants smile. Thedford
strode briskly up to the prescription counter just like any other of
the townspeople. "Need a bottle of aspirin," he announced.

Doc Bodkin reached inside the glass door engraved with the
winged staff with a coiled snake, associated with the medical profession. The oak cabinet with the elegant glass door was given to
him by his parents when he graduated from pharmacy school. He
extracted a small bottle of little white tablets and handed them to
the miserly customer. Thedford pocketed the bottle and, after

paying, walked briskly through the front doors in the direction of his home just off Toadsuck's main street. In an unusually brisk pace, Doc Bodkin followed Thedford out of the store. "Wait up, Mr. Goforth," Thedford heard behind him as he hurried home with relief for his nagging headache.

"What is it, Doc?" he asked, turning to see the doctor pursuing him vigorously.

"I made a mistake," said the town druggist in an urgent tone of voice! "You ordered aspirin, didn't you?" asked the well-liked pharmacist.

"Sure did, Doc, got a nagging headache that ain't getting any better standing hear jawing with you," replied the town's famous tightwad, becoming agitated at being delayed!

"I made a big mistake when I filled your order," said Doc Bodkin. "Instead of aspirin, I gave you cyanide," said the apologetic druggist.

"What's the difference?" asked the miserly Thedford. "Two dollars and fifty cents," replied the druggist, aware of Thedford's penny-pinching ways.

On the Wagon, Almost

The old Toadsuck Saloon' customers were a potpourri of North Texas men of all ages and each having a hollow leg in varying capacity! Samuel Fenimore, the saloon's long-time bartender had heard, he thought, "just about every kind of story from the saddest to the funniest" that one could imagine. But that was before he met Titus Tabor, a drummer from back East, who sold kitchen ware to general stores from St. Louis to El Paso.

The day he first stepped off the T&P in Toadsuck and lugged his sample case into the Toadsuck Saloon, Sam knew he had a regular customer. A bit more polished than the saloon's regular crowd of elbow benders, Titus could drink with the best of them. His almost weekly trip through Toadsuck provided Sam with a puzzling, but profitable, routine. Each time Titus bellied up to the oak bar, Sam could count on the same order. "Gimmi two whiskeys and two beers," Titus requested. He then proceeded to down the four drinks in enough time that would permit him to board the outbound train. He talked little and left Sam a generous tip, which was more than the friendly barkeep could expect from most rather rough-hewn locals. Sam knew he could expect Titus back in about a week with the exact same order and routine consumption before departing with his sample case headed for the next customer.

This routine, Sam said, continued on weekly for about two years. One can understand Sam's bewilderment when one warm day in June the train deposited Titus and his sample case on the depot platform where he stayed a few minutes before he made his usual appearance in the Toadsuck Saloon. After Sam had greeted the drummer and inquired about sales and his family, Samuel was confronted with the surprise of his career behind the bar in Toadsuck.

He was just about to draw the usual two beers to go with the two glasses of whiskey he already poured for his customer when Titus held up his hand motioning him to stop. Only one beer and one whiskey this time, Sam, said the drummer. Taken aback by the drummer's drastic change from his usual order, Sam was compelled to ask about the customer's change in habit! "For the past years you have placed the same order of two whiskeys and two beers, which you drank. Do you mind explaining your sudden departure from this order?"

"Glad to oblige you, Sam," Titus said, with a faint smile creasing his face. "You see, it's this way. Several years ago one of my best friends died. We had hoisted many a drink together. Before he died he made me promise that after he was gone, when I had a drink, I'd drink one for him, too! So, you see, when I asked for the two whiskeys and two beers, one of them was for my friend."

"I can fully understand that," said Sam, with a glimmer of a tear in his eyes. "Mighty thoughtful gesture, I would have to say. But why today did you order only one whiskey and one beer?"

"Well," said Titus, "those were for my friend. I have quit drinking."

True Confession at the "Bubba Table"

If you needed to find the menfolk in Toadsuck between the hours of 6:00 A.M. and lunchtime, all you had to do was stop in at Quince Baker's Main Street Café. There in the back corner of the café the town's good ol' boys gathered at what was called the "Bubba Table." This was especially true during hunting season. It was in this congregation that each man could freely, if not always believed, elaborate on his hunting and fishing prowess. All this accompanied by gallons of coffee strong enough to float a horseshoe, and plate after plate of biscuits and cream gravy. All served by a very tolerant Louvella Bledsoe. Annie Myrtle Quince, the café's morning cook, once said that the men "could eat a number three washtub of her cream gravy if there was enough black coffee to wash it down."

It was in this setting one morning just after duck season had opened that Clifford Denley made his neck-saving confession. During his second helping of biscuits and gravy Clifford, proudly wearing his camouflage jacket, stood up and in a loud and boisterous fashion proclaimed how he had, on the first day of the season, shot 35 ducks! "And," he proclaimed to all his peers, "on the second day, I got 45 ducks!" Not content with this display of manliness, Clifford, quite loudly presented a $50 wager that "today I'll bag another 35 ducks."

Just as Clifford took his seat before more of Annie Myrtle's biscuits and cream gravy, a stranger sitting at a nearby table who had been nursing a cup of coffee during Clifford's loud proclamation of his hunting successes, stood up. "Do you know who I am?" he asked, addressing his question to Clifford.

"No," replied Toadsuck's Bubba of the morning.

"Well," continued the stranger, "I'm the county's new game warden."

Clifford, now looking a little peaked, as if he was coming down with the flu, asked the man, "Do you know who I am?"

"I'm afraid I don't," replied the stranger, who was fast becoming unwelcome in the town's café.

"Well," continued Clifford, in a loud but not so boisterous tone of voice, "I'm the biggest liar in Grayson County!"

Cleanliness is Next to Godliness

Although its author is unknown, it is almost a universally accepted adage that cleanliness ranks right up there with one's spirituality! This, I can say without fear of correction, was the case in most homes in Toadsuck. Often having little except their pride, the womenfolk in Toadsuck would rather be caught dead than to have their house found untidy. This is why Ruby Lee Puckett would have liked to have found a hole to crawl into when her second grader, Billy Ed, unwittingly revealed one of her deepest, darkest, domestic secrets.

Rily and Ruby Lee were very proud of their children, especially Billy Ed, who excelled in school and found Sunday school at the Mount Zion Baptist Church a fun way to spend Sunday morning. This pride in Billy Ed was truly put to the test one Saturday when Ruby Lee and Riley agreed to make homemade ice cream for the Mt. Zion Woman's Bible Class.

"Why is it," parents always ask, "that your kids pick a time when company comes to find a way to put the entire family to shame?" This was a particularly damaging occasion, for one of Toadsuck's most infamous gossips, Frieda Nell Bledsoe, was in attendance.

Riley always said Sister Bledsoe had indentations under her arms from hanging over backyard fences exchanging gossip with her neighbors. How Riley knew what Frieda Nell had under her arms was never a question broached in the Puckett household!

On this particular day, Billy Ed was quietly listening to the adults talk about topics to be taken under consideration for the Bible class when he interrupted long enough to ask his mother a pretty serious question for a ten-year-old. "Mother, last week in Sunday school the teacher said "We come from dust and when we die we go back to dust." Do you think that is true?"

"That's what the Bible teaches," replied Ruby Lee, proud that her son at least paid attention to the Sunday school lessons.

"Then," continued the bright little boy, "there's something you ought to know. Yesterday my ball rolled under the bed and when I went under to get it, I noticed that someone was under there, either coming or going!"

"Little Pitchers Have Big Ears!"

The Bullock kids always loved to spend the summers on their grandfather's small, Bar-None Ranch just outside of Toadsuck. The opportunity to ride horses and just roam the pastures unfettered by shoes and school was a treat for Luke and his sister, Mae Ruth. Grandfather, C. W. "Buck" Shotts, tolerated the kid's endless questions and spoiled them rotten. The kids returned home with fond memories that would have to tide them over until next year. Some of their best were created in the evenings just after supper when Grandpa Shotts would sit out on the big gallery porch and spin yarns about his youth on a West Texas ranch. One such evening almost brought about a deep split in the family.

Grandpa Shotts had just pointed out a most impressive white tail buck deer that quietly strolled leisurely across his front pasture to the delight of the children. Luke turned to his grandfather and said "Grandpa, will you make a noise like a frog?"

The elderly man thought the young boy was thinking about the frogs that he had seen in the stock tank on the ranch. "Luke, said Mr. Shotts, I'm too full to make a noise like a frog, maybe later."

Time passed quietly as the three sat together on the enormous gallery porch. About a quarter hour later Luke interrupted his grandfather in the midst of a story he was telling and asked," Grandpa Shotts, are you still too full to make a noise like a frog?"

The patient old man brushed Luke off one more time with a lame excuse as to why he couldn't make a noise like a frog. Luke and Mae Ruth must have sat for two hours taking in the stories of their adored grandfather. The stillness of the evening was broken by the voice of their grandmother calling the kids to bed. "Before

we go to bed, Grandpa, won't you please make a noise like a frog?" asked Luke with a tone bordering on urgency!

The boy's tone of voice caused their grandfather to ask, "Why, Luke, is it so important that I make a noise like a frog?"

"Well, said the young boy, we love this place, and we heard Mama tell Daddy that when you croak the ranch will be ours!"

If it Was Important, it Must Have Been in Texas!

Miss Mamie Cowan had been teaching most of her thirty-odd years and thought she had heard it all. But that was until the Christmas of 1933 when she was teaching fifth grade history at the Toadsuck Elementary School. Wanting to make the class interesting enough to hold her students' interest, and knowing that the season had captured the minds of every child in Toadsuck, she took this opportunity to work the Christmas season into her history class.

What Miss Cowan had not taken into consideration was that in her class was Joe Edd Baker, whose father worked as the county agent for the Texas Department of Agriculture. All Joe Edd heard from his father was how great Texas was. "Great in all respects!" His father's loyalty to Texas, both as an employer and as a part of the biggest state in the union, was preached to the Baker family from morning to night. So it was no wonder that Joe Edd fairly oozed with Texas, like it was a religion rather than a state. "If it was great, it must have happened in Texas!" was the philosophy in the Baker household.

So when Miss Cowan asked if anyone in the class knew where Jesus was born, it was to be expected that the first hand to be raised was Joe Edd Baker's. He almost stood on his tiptoes as he extended his right arm like the school's flagpole. When no other hands went up, Joe Edd, eager to show his prowess in history, breathed a sigh of relief. Miss Cowan has to call on me first, he thought. Sure enough, the teacher had little choice but to call on the eager student, practically purple in the face from holding his breath in anticipation.

"Well, Joe Edd, you seem to be the only one in class today who knows where Jesus was born, where was the Christ child born?"

"In Longview," said Joe Edd, almost shouting!

"No," Joe Edd, "I'm afraid that's not correct," replied the surprised teacher.

"It must have been Lufkin, then," stammered Joe Edd, in a positive voice.

"Not correct," said an unbelieving Miss Cowan. "Joe Edd," she said, as she looked the lad squarely in his eager face, "Jesus was born in Palestine."

"Well," said Joe Edd, smugly, "I knew it was somewhere in East Texas."

A Charlie By Any Other Name

Ida Fay Lingle, unlike the other Lingle girls, suffered from a bad reputation. Ida Fay was somewhat boy crazy from the time she graduated from the Toadsuck Elementary School. Her high school days were anything but boring for the "belle of the ball." Being called a "pushover" by the eleven members of the

Toadsuck football team and the infield of the baseball team, not to mention the winner of last year's declamation contest, only made Ida Fay feel more feminine.

And Ida Fay couldn't feel satisfied just being popular with the young men of Toadsuck. She seemed to thrive on getting serious with each of the men who pursued her. She kept track of her steady fellers like gunfighters of old notched their guns after a killing. Those who added Ida Fay to their list of conquests more than once usually ended up being paraded down the aisle, as the star attraction at this year's "Ida Fay's catch of the year" wedding. Ida Fay once got a call from Guiness World Record Book advising her that she easily qualified for making more parents in-laws than anyone on record.

Her many unions, as one could expect, produced a house full of kids. During the 1922 census, the census taker asked Ida Fay, "How many children do you have?"

"I got six boys," replied Toadsuck's perennial bride.

"And," asked the government census representative, "what are their names?"

"Charlie," answered Ida Fay as her eyes gave the nice-looking census taker the once over.

"I need the names of each of the boys," he continued.

"That is the name of each of the boys," insisted Ida Fay, this time batting her heavily mascarad eyelashes.

The census taker, awestruck by Ida Fay's answer as well as her "come hither" look, queried. "If each of the boys are all named Charlie, when you call them, how do they know which one you want?"

"If I want a particular one, I call him by his last name."

Fine Print Ain't Necessarily So Fine!

When the T&P bypassed Toadsuck, it sent residents scurrying away in the direction of the railhead. Businesses, especially those like Clint Moffat's family diner, were thrown into a state of reorganization, another more business-like way of saying "panic."

Clint had been serving good, wholesome blue-plate specials to folks in and around Toadsuck for years. He was respected as an honest, congenial businessman and friend. Billy Jack McCarty had been parking his hay hauling truck in front of Clint's diner at least three times a week as long as anyone could remember. Like most working men, Billy Jack knew he could count on Gladys Feeney serving up a heapin' portion of biscuits and cream gravy for breakfast every morning. Clint's cooks had never been tight when it came to putting portions of wholesome food on a workingman's plate. And, nobody complained about Clint's moderate prices. But with folks fleeing the fast diminishing town, Clint had to think of himself for a change!

It was LaNell Moffat who came up with the diner's big promotion that became the talk of what was left of the town. One Saturday at lunchtime, Billy Jack walked in the diner and took his seat on the stool nearest the window where LaNell, the diner's star and only waitress, turned in the customers' orders. That way he could see when his order was ready and prod LaNell into action if the orders sat too long under the diner's newfangled heating lamps, which seemed to make the cream gravy clabber and get lumpy.

Billy Jack was smitten in amazement at the huge new banner he saw strung up on the wall just above the window to the kitchen. Had Clint suddenly inherited money? he wondered to himself. The colorful sign read,

All You Can Eat for a Dollar

The November chill prompted Billy Jack to order a bowl of Clint's popular "red-eye" chili. This would tide the hard-working farmer over until he could get home to some of Mae Ruth's delectable pot roast she had mumbled something about as he left for the day.

"LaNell, he fairly screamed over the noise produced by the customers and kitchen help in the confines of the small diner. "Gimmi a bowl of that steaming red-eye, please!" It wasn't long before the waitress, with an eye for tips, sat the chili and a plate of saltines before the farmer, whose growling innards betrayed his noontime hunger.

After wolfing down the chili into which he had crumbled a fistful of the saltines, he caught Clint's attention as he stepped from behind the cash register long enough to greet a couple of regular customer. "I saw your new sign and I'd like a refill on my bowl of chili."

"Don't give refills on coffee, much less food orders," said the owner in a matter-of-fact tone of voice.

"But," protested Billy Jack, "your sign says, 'All you can eat for a dollar.'"

"Well" replied Clint, "That's all you can eat for a dollar!"

A normally easy-going Billy Jack slid off the counter stool and walked briskly and certainly wiser out of the diner. He mumbled something to an arriving customer about "Beware of false advertising" as he headed back to work. He cursed the T&P for making such nice folks turn to greed to try to save their vanishing businesses. He didn't return to his favorite eating place until Clint Moffat took down the gaudy promotional banner. Clint and

LaNell never let Billy Jack leave without asking, "Did you get your dollar's worth?" Clint's Diner survived the town's transition, and Billy Jack still patronizes the place despite being the butt of the "All you can eat" joke!

Out of the Mouths of Babes

Children everywhere have been known to say things that can be embarassing. And Edna Sue Witherspoon was not the only Toadsuck child who was indirectly responsible for bringing some measure of embarrassment to their parents. Her childish misunderstanding of her mother is still talked about at the First United Methodist Church. Or at least it was last time Nadine and I attended.

One morning in the Piggly Wiggly store, Mr. Timpkins asked Edna Sue if she was Matthew Witherspoon's little girl? Edna Sue proudly affirmed that she was. Later back home Edna Sue's mother, who had overheard the conversation, called the pretty little girl aside and said, "You shouldn't say you are Mr. Witherspoon's daughter. When someone wants to know your name, you should say I'm Edna Sue Witherspoon." It seemed to the girl's mother that her instructions were perfectly clear.

Next Sunday at Sunday school proved Mrs. Witherspoon wrong. The new Sunday school teacher asked Edna Sue, "Aren't you Matthew Witherspoon's little girl?"

Edna Sue innocently turned this inquiry into a community topic of conversation when she answered, "I thought I was, but Mama said I wasn't."

No Dog-Catcher Needed!

Elsie Fay Higgins and her husband Rudy have been married over forty years. Rudy still looks handsome despite his sixty-six years and his salt and pepper hair. One day in Leo's Toadsuck Diner, Gussie Nell Davis, one of the diner's popular waitresses, gave Rudy a little tweak on the cheek as she delivered his check. This little show of innocent freshness did not go unnoticed by Bessie Mae Tindel, which was nothing unusual for Bessie Mae, who was known for sticking her unwanted nose into other folk's business.

A few days later at the Toadsuck Pay and Tote Grocery store, Bessie and Elsie Fay came face to face in front of the meat counter where Elsie Fay waited patiently for Horace Brinkley to put out some fresh hog jowls, which were destined for a big pot of Elsie's prize-winning purple-hull peas. Bessie Mae's philosophy about a bit of juicy gossip was, "What good is gossip if it can't be shared with your friends?"

Upon seeing Elsie Fay, the incident involving Rudy and the "brazen hussy" at Leo's diner was just too good to pass up! "What shameful conduct on the part of that Gussie Nell," said Bessie Mae. "Don't that make you want to just yank a handful of her peroxide hair right out, or maybe some of Rudy's?"

"No," answered Elsie Fay in a calm tone of voice. "Everyone in Toadsuck knows that Rudy, sweet as he is, is like the dog that chased cars."

"And," answered Bessie with a puzzled, and disappointed look on her face, "just what do you mean?"

"Well, we had a neighbor who had a dog that chased cars. One day Rudy asked the neighbor, 'Aren't you afraid for your dog to chase cars?' To which the neighbor replied 'Not at all, if he caught one, he wouldn't know what to do with it!'"

Bessie Mae, who stood there watching her latest bit of gossip go up in smoke, walked away with a face that nearly touched the floor!

"Sticks and Stones May Break My Bones"

Every time I hear a child repeat this time-worm rhyme in defense of someone's name calling, I think to myself, They just didn't know about Tommy Lee and Jo Etta Babcock! The two had been sweethearts as long as anyone in Toadsuck could remember. The ink was barely dry on Superintendent Wheelock's name on their graduation diploma when they found themselves standing "Before God, and in the presence of this company." in the little Holy Shepherd Pentecostal Church being bound together "'til death do you part."

All the young couple knew about themselves was what they had observed in the classroom and what they had learned on weekends in Tommy Lee's six-year-old International pickup, when they drove to watch the sunset at the pond next to Harold Denby's sawmill. And that was more than either wanted to admit. Nevertheless, they felt they were quite ready to face the future in each other's arms.

One thing Tommy Lee had failed to learn, either in his classes with Jo Etta or in his old International, was that a man never openly belittles the sanctity of holy wedlock if he truly values his bride, regardless of how long they have been man and wife!

Neither could ever remember the exact incident that initiated the exchange of words that resulted in their becoming a statistic in Toadsuck's Domestic Court. Tommy Lee recalled it all started when Jo Etta "raised cane when I wanted to invest in a new Evenrude for my aluminum fishing boat. I asserted myself by reminding Jo Etta that the man was the head of the house. She retorted by somewhat firmly announcing that was correct, but the woman was the neck, and the neck always turned the head."

Things in the new household rocked along fairly smooth following this unexpected interruption of marital bliss until one evening about two months later when Jo Etta, in what amounted to a mild peace offering, suggested that Tommy Lee invite a few of his buddies over for a domino party. This, she thought, might give his friends a chance to see the Holy Bonds of Matrimony in its best light. She even consented to Tommy Lee's request to buy a full case of beer as an example of how acceptable married life can be. This added ingredient only served to galvanize Tommy Lee's pent up resentment of his wife's high-handedness in their still-fresh marriage.

Jo Etta watched the men as they exchanged fishing and hunting stories with a camaraderie that only men seem to foster. She kept herself busy in the couple's small kitchen popping popcorn, in hopes of making Tommy Lee proud to show off his newly acquired domestic life. Through the laughter generated by a few slightly off-colored jokes shared by the men, Jo Etta was able to hear Tommy Lee's buddies compliment him for his newfound lifestyle. This was very gratifying to Jo Etta, who felt a little like a shrew for coming down so hard on her new husband about the new motor for his boat.

Her remorseful condition was short-lived when, as the skillet was emptied of another batch of popcorn, in the quietness that followed she heard Sam Blevins ask Tommy Lee what he thought of married life. Intent on hearing her husband's answer, Jo Etta cracked the kitchen door slightly and gave the conversation her full attention.

This, like permitting Tommy Lee to buy the case of beer, was her second mistake! What she heard violated all her senses, as well as, she thought, their solemn marriage vows. Tommy Lee, somewhat in a laughing tone of voice, replied, "Married life is like taking a hot bath, once you get used to it, it's not so hot!"

Stunned by the somewhat alcohol-induced laughter that followed, a very disillusioned Jo Etta, without so much as a "by-your-leave" to their guests, slunk off like a hurt animal to their bedroom. This was to be the last party of any kind to be held in the Babcock residence.

Following a morning of coolness between the two, the likes of which could only be compared to the winter of 1916, things between the newly wedded Babcocks went from bad to bitter! Their resulting appearance in Toadsuck's Domestic Court was inevitable. So, whoever believes the words to "Sticks and stones" was never married and has a lot to learn about domestic relations!

Evil May Just Be a Point of View!

Sixty-year-old Mavis Harkey was one of the first tenants in Toadsuck's first apartment complex. Since had Leroy passed away, this was a perfect setup for Mavis. Her kids insisted that she live in a place where no yard work was required. A company maintenance man was available to take care of minor repair jobs.

There was no longer a need to
bother the kids when something
needed fixing. Mavis had good
neighbors who all looked out
for each other. Then, as they
say, "Up jumped the devil!"

One day Mavis, a prudish widow, called
Grayson County Sheriff Ted Blevins to report an offensive case
of indecent conduct. "Every morning," she began her call, "the
man in the apartment directly across the courtyard from me goes
into his bathroom and removes his clothes without pulling the
shade. It happens about the time I'm fixing my breakfast, and I
am so shocked at what I see, I can barely do my cooking. Surely
you can make him move, or charge him with some crime to teach
him some manners."

"Well," interrupted the sheriff, "we can't do anything unless
we catch him in the act of doing something improper."

"Won't be hard to do," injected Mavis. "You just have one of
your men at my house in the morning at 7:30, and I'll show you
why I am so incensed at this pervert's blatant exposing of
himself."

The next morning just as Mavis was fixing her morning coffee, a knock at her door signaled the arrival of the uniformed
deputy assigned to give Mavis some relief from her embarrassing
neighbor. Mavis immediately took the deputy into her kitchen.
"Now," she said, pointing to a window in the apartment directly
across from hers, "you watch that window and in about ten minutes the man will come in and undress without pulling down his
shade."

Sure enough, right on Mavis' schedule, a well-built young
man entered the lighted bathroom and began to remove his

clothes as he stood in front of his mirror. The deputy, after watching several minutes, went to Mrs. Harkey. "I see what you are saying about the man undressing, Mrs. Harkey, but you can only see the man from his shoulders down to his waist."

With this, Mavis pointed to a kitchen chair and exclaimed rather forcefully, "You just stand up in that chair and look, young man!"

A Story Anybody Could See Through!

When I was a kid growing up just outside of Toadsuck, Oscar Pudley, as far as I know, was the only man with a "glass eye," as artificial eyes were called then, in Toadsuck or maybe the whole county. Most folks who lost an eye just wore a black patch over the missing eye. Glass eyes were much too expensive for the average person.

But when Oscar lost his eye after the rim blew off a wheel while he was changing a tire at the Magnolia station, the Magnolia folks saw to it that Oscar was sent all the way to Dallas to be treated and fitted with an artificial eye. We all thought it mighty decent of the folks at Magnolia to give Oscar this special treatment, and to make him a minor celebrity in Toadsuck.

I remember one day when Rufe Barlow was in the county inspecting the KATY railroad bridges, he ran into Oscar at the Fina station where he was relieving Riley Puckett, who was off sick with a busted collar bone. Rufe hadn't seen Oscar since he got his new eye, although, like most folks in Grayson County, he had heard about it. During a lull in business Rufe called old Oscar aside and asked him, "Oscar, what is your new eye made out of?"

According to "Fats" Wilson, who was putting water in his radiator at the time, Oscar, with as straight a face as one can imagine, looked right in the face of Rufe and said, "It's made out of glass, you fool, otherwise how would I be able to see through it?"

Fast Thinkers Start Young!

We have given Billy Earl Blevens due credit for being quick on his feet when it comes to thinking fast at the appropriate time, such as when he got his truck stuck under the KATY Railroad bridge just south of Denison while driving for the Toadsuck Nationwide Freight Company. But just so you won't think Billy Earl's quick-wittedness came late in life, we want to share a story his father-in-law, Jess Peabody, told about Billy Earl when he was courtin' Jess' middle daughter, Mary Pearline.

Jess said he had strict rules that his girls were not to be brought home later than ten thirty when they were out on a date. He said one evening he looked in on Mary Pearline's room at ten o'clock, while she was out with Billy Earl at a school dance over in Brinkley Switch. Finding an empty bed, he returned to bed to await the return of the couple. He said he was awakened by the closing of the front door, and he slipped on his robe and quietly made his way downstairs to greet Billy Earl, fully intending on laying into him about keeping Mary out so late.

Jess said he turned to Billy Earl and said rather brusquely, "Didn't I just hear the clock strike four as I came down the stairs?"

"Yes, you sure did," replied the girl's suitor, with trembling knees. "It was just about to strike ten when I grabbed the gong so it wouldn't disturb you," answered the fast thinking Blevens boy.

Mary Pearline's father said he wished he'd thought of that when he was courtin'. Yes, Billy Earl's quick-wittedness was a trait he had learned early in life.

"There Ain't No Free Lunches"

The young doctor who replaced 'ol Doc Mckinzie had hardly got his office set up when he started learning medical lessons in Toadsuck. But, to his credit, he had a few lessons of his own up his sleeve.

It wasn't long before local folks began taking advantage of his friendliness. He could hardly cross the street to Clif's barbershop for a haircut without getting stopped for some free medical advice. If you looked close when you saw the doctor out of his office you could see one of your Toadsuck neighbors close by gesturing to all parts of their body. You knew right then they were in the process of trying to avoid a visit to the doctor's office by describing their ailments in hopes of getting a street diagnosis for free.

Lemuel Trobridge had been "fleshy," a polite word folks used that meant fat, for the better part of his adult life. Ol' Doc Mckinzie passed it off to Lem as bad genes rather than make Lem mad about his steam shovel eating habits or his wife's cooking having more starch than a Chinese laundry. But when Lem started getting deep heartburn even when he ate oatmeal or cotton candy at the Grayson County 4H Fair, he got to worrying something fierce. Fierce enough to buttonhole the doc in front of the feed store one day and ask him his advice. He obviously wasn't worried enough to pay for a visit to the doctor's office. The doctor told Lem he needed to lose forty pounds or face a heart attack.

"But, Doc, how can a guy who loves to eat like I do lose forty pounds? That's like asking a circus elephant to give up free peanuts!"

"Exercise is the only answer," said the doc, without batting an eye. "And I don't mean increasing the number of trips you walk to the domino parlor," he emphasized. "If you really want to lose forty pounds, you need to walk ten miles a day for one hundred days."

The new doctor didn't hear a word from Lem for weeks. Then, his conversation with Lem totally forgotten, one day out of the blue he gets a long-distance call from his obese patient. "Well, Doc, you really got me in a mess!"

"What kind of mess?" inquired the town doctor.

"I followed your advice and walked ten miles a day for one hundred days."

"And, did you lose weight?" asked the doc.

"Yes," said Lem, "I lost forty pounds."

"Great!" said the surprised physician. "Then why are we in a mess?"

"Well now I'm a thousand miles from home," said Lem.

The Power of Suggestion

One warm day about noon a big burly cowpoke rode into Toadsuck. The stranger tied his bay mare to the well-worn hitching rail in front of the original Toadsuck Saloon. He briskly strode inside and asked Quinton Kelley, the barkeep, for a beer.

Some of the locals had a habit of picking on strangers. When the stranger finished his beer, he walked outside and noticed his horse had been stolen. He set the doors to swinging violently, as he slammed against them with all his weight and returned inside. Once in the saloon, the big stranger flipped his revolver out of its holster and fired a shot into the beveled mirror that ran the length of the bar. Then in a boisterous voice he said, "Somebody has taken my horse! I'm going to drink another beer and if it ain't back where I tied it when I'm done, I'm going to be forced to do what I done in San Antonio last year! And," he bellowed in unmistakably angry tones, "I don't like having to do what I done in San Antonio, last year!" All the while, the stranger nervously fingered his holstered revolver.

Quinton couldn't help but notice that even the town rowdies standing nearby shifted restlessly. The big burly stranger drank his second beer and then turned to leave. As he turned, those standing between him and the saloon's green swinging doors seemed to part, much like the Red Sea parted for Moses, leaving a clear path for the cowboy to exit. When he got outside, the stranger found his horse had been returned and tied exactly where he left it.

Quinton, who had followed his customer outside noted the return of his horse. "Say," Quinton asked, in a most friendly voice, "it's really none of my business, but what did you do in San Antonio?"

The stranger, still fingering his six-shooter turned to the bar-keeper and said, "I had to walk home."

You Asked For It

"Greasy" Edgar Plimpton, the mechanic at the Toadsuck Fina station was known for not mincing words with anyone, that is except when it came to quoting prices for his mechanical work. His habit of speaking his mind may have cost him a new customer when the Reverend Edger Whitesides moved to Toadsuck to pas-tor the Poplar Street Christian Church.

The new pastor brought his car to Edgar for a minor tune-up job. Before leaving the Fina station, Brother Whitesides asked Edgar, or "Greasy Ed," as he was called, what the charges would be. The new preacher left himself wide open when, in asking, he added "Remember, I'm a poor preacher."

Edgar's reply was enough to cost him any further business from the pastor. Greasy Ed replied, "Yes, I am aware of that, I heard you preach last Sunday."

Trick or Treat in Toadsuck!

Halloween in Toadsuck was the one time in the year when much in the way of shenanigans were overlooked. It was expected that outhouses would be overturned and a wagon would be disassembled and reassembled on the roof of its owner's barn. But Winnie and Arlis Winterbottom will never forget the Hallow-een of 1923. We wouldn't even be able to relate the story had not Winnie, years later, confided in Caroline Harris at an Eastern Star bingo night. The old maid editor of the *Toadsuck Sentinel* found the story too good to keep to herself. Winnie confessed the Halloween prank that backfired after one too many trips to the lodge's spiked punch bowl.

Winnie said that she and Arlis made plans to attend the Toadsuck Volunteer Fire Department's fund-raising Halloween dance, which had the reputation of being "a man's night to howl" type of party. Winnie said that on the night of the much anticipated party she came down with a blinding headache. She insisted that Arlis go by himself, although he politely argued that he would gladly stay home with her. She knew how much he wanted to go to the party, as most of his male friends would be there. And he had already put together a humdinger of a costume. He was certain to win one of the prizes offered.

Later, Winnie, after taking two aspirin and a short nap, awoke feeling much better. She decided she would go to the party, and since she knew what Arlis' costume was, this would give her a chance to see how her husband acted when she was not with him.

Wearing a costume that he had not seen, she arrived in the fire hall in time to catch Arlis dancing with that hussy Mable Shook, the switchboard operator at the Toadsuck clinic. Arlis seemed, Winnie said, to have learned several new ways to hold a dance partner. His hands were busy exploring Mable's charms. But, she noticed, his technique seemed not to be limited to Miss Shook! Winnie said that Arlis danced close enough to Betty Lou Sykes to rub the glitter off her fairy princess costume.

Then came Winnie's chance. She waited until her husband escorted his next dance partner to her seat and then she moved in for the domestic kill! Surely

Arlis, who didn't recognize his wife, having never seen her costume, would want to dance with the pretty new arrival. Right she was! Arlis extended his glitter-covered hand and asked Winnie for a dance.

They had barely circled the floor once when Arlis began to let his hands wander. But Winnie's real shock came just as the dance was about to end. In the darkened room, Arlis whispered a seductive invitation to join him in the parking lot for a back seat romp in the hay in his car. Winnie nodded an acceptance.

After returning from the romantic rendezvous in the car, Winnie quickly got her wrap and went home. The next morning she confronted her husband "Well, did you dance a lot at the party last night?"

"Hardly danced at all," replied Arlis.

"Well what did you do to have fun?" Winnie asked.

"Me and Pete and a couple of guys played poker most of the night."

"I'm really sorry you didn't have much fun," lamented Winnie.

"Well," said Arlis, "wait till I tell you what happened to the guy I loaned my costume to!"

Fame Can Be Flighty

It was Billy Bob's higher (for the Toadsuck region) education in Denison that helped land him his job as a long haul driver for Toadsuck Nationwide Freight Company. Billy Bob was considered one of Toadsuck's better minds. But the young man was soon to find out that fame can be a very temporary thing. It took only one occasion for Billy Bob's educational prowess to vanish like a summer dust devil.

It all happened one summer morning when Toadsuck's popular barber, Clif Pearson, started to Oklahoma City to see his ailing mother. Clif turned off FM 1225 just in time to see Billy Bob's truck going north on Highway 62. Ol' Billy Bob was rared back in the driver's seat like an engineer on the KATY Flyer. Clif followed his fellow townsman as he sped along the state highway in the direction of the Red River.

Billy Bob's reputation would have remained intact had it not been for his strange conduct. Clif later told his wife, Opal, that after about five miles Billy Bob pulled to the shoulder of the road, slid out of the driver's seat, and walked to the rear of his truck where he pulled an axe handle from under his toolbox. Clif told Opal how Toadsuck's brainiest resident then started walking back to his seat in the truck's cab, banging the aluminum side of the trailer with his wooden club. "Billy Bob banged the truck vigorously, making enough noise to awaken the dead," said the barber. He then took his seat and continued on his way, with Clif close behind.

Clif related how he followed the big trailer truck for about five miles when, once again, Billy Bob pulled the big rig to the shoulder of the highway and stopped. Clif, too, stopped a few hundred feet behind Billy Bob's trailer. He watched in amazement, he told Opal, as Billy Bob slid from his seat and walked briskly to the rear of the trailer and retrieved his wooden club. After pausing long enough to catch his breath, the driver walked slowly back to his seat, banging lustily on the side of the trailer as he walked.

Hearing Billy Bob start his engine, Clif put his car into motion and started his pursuit of the big aluminum trailer once again. By this time, Clif was beside himself with curiosity at Billy Bob's strange antics. He was determined to follow his friend all the way to St. Louis, if necessary, to find out why the truck was taking such a beating at the hands of its driver. His curiosity was to be satisfied within the hour as, right on schedule, after another five miles, Billy Bob pulled his truck to the side of the highway and stopped.

Sure enough, while Clif watched in utter amazement, the pride of Toadsuck stepped from his cab and made his way to the rear of the truck. After taking his club in hand, he made his way back to the driver's seat, flailing away at the trailer's sides. Unwilling to wait another minute for an answer to Billy Bob's puzzling antics, Clif left his car and caught up with Billy Bob as he was about to drive away. He point-blank, without beating around the bush, asked Billy Bob why he was stopping every five miles and beating on the sides of his trailer. His friend looked him straight in the eye and explained his strange conduct.

"You see, Clif," he said, pointing to some numbers stenciled on the side of the trailer, "This trailer has a maximum legal cargo weight of 6,000 pounds. At my last stop the customer loaded on 12,000 pounds of parakeets, and to be legal, I have to keep half of the birds flying at all times!"

"Keep Your Fork"

Although a small community, Toadsuck was blessed by having several churches. The folks in Toadsuck had one commonality. They seemed to all have a deep faith in the Almighty and the part he played in their meager but fulfilling existence.

One story told by the pastor of the Toadsuck Methodist Church was about one of the congregation's older sisters who had been diagnosed with a terminal illness. Knowing that she had only a few months to live, she began to "get things in order," as rural folks are wont to do. She asked that her pastor come by her rural folks are wont to do. She asked that her pastor come by her house to discuss her final wishes. She discussed with him the songs she would like to have sung at her funeral, as well as the scriptures she wanted read. She also said she wished to be buried with her favorite, well-worn Bible. She even told him the dress she wished to be buried in.

The preacher was about to leave when the woman remembered something else that was very important to her. Her final wish was very Toadsuckian in nature. "I want to be buried with a fork in my right hand," she said. The departing pastor paused and turned to her with a quizzical expression. "I can see that my wish surprises you," the church member remarked in a weak, but resolved voice. "Let me explain," said the woman. "In all my years of attending church socials and potluck dinners, when the dishes from the main course were being cleared, someone would inevitably lean over and say, 'Keep you fork.' This was always my favorite part, as I knew something better was coming … like velvety chocolate cake or someone's deep-dish apple pie. Something with 'stick-to-your-rib substance.' So I want folks to see me there in the casket with my fork in my hand, and I want them to wonder, 'What's with the fork?' Then I want you to tell them that I just wanted to be prepared because I knew the best was yet to come."

The pastor's eyes welled with tears as he leaned over and kissed the faithful church member goodbye, as he knew the old woman had a better grasp of Heaven than most in his congregation. She did know that something better was waiting for her, and she was prepared!

The afternoon of her funeral, he did hear several who slowly passed by the casket wonder aloud, "Why the fork?" The next Sunday during his sermon he explained about his unusual conversation with the church member. He told them how he could not stop thinking about the fork, and he bet they wouldn't either.

That day, after Sunday dinner, many who attended that small church couldn't help but look down at their forks!

Beyond Bickering

I guess every town and community has a couple whose married bliss has turned to blisters! Their fussin' goes beyond the spats that can be expected in most marriages. Those who are neighbors to such couples generally have unsolicited ring-side seats to the loud and sometimes violent "squabbles" of these parties in a less than blissful marriage. Toadsuck was no exception when it came to coexistence that was less than peaceful.

Hiram and Sudie Pearl Crowder didn't grow up in the Toadsuck area but moved their trailer home to a 50x50-foot vacant lot when Hiram lost his job at the caliche quarry near Buxite, Oklahoma. According to Winfred Higgins, who lived on the lot adjoining the Crowders, he first noticed the couple's bickering when Hiram came home from his new job at Denley's "Donuts By the Dozen" shop in downtown Toadsuck and found Sudie Pearl with her hair done up on rollers, "big as a number two can of hominy."

An embarrassed Hiram explained later. Hiram told Winfred that he thought Sudie Pearl was acting pretty uppity since she had been asked to write a monthly newsletter for the North Texas Trailerhouse Association. She started watching them daytime talk shows like "Eva Gabor speaks to middle-class women."

Hiram said she saw one of Eva's guests on the show with curls so big you could spray 'em hard and watch TV in bed without a neck pillow. "All Sudie Pearl needs is more TV," Hiram commented. The girl on the show got her big curls by rolling them on a Heinz Tomato can.

But this was only the first big argument. The bickering escalated, according to Winfred, into some real knock-down drag-outs that would have made a professional mud wrestler jealous. "After getting better acquainted," said Winfred, "I found it was not all Sudie Pearl's fault." Hiram claimed to be a practicing witch and bragged about doing away with several pets of neighbors back in Oklahoma. He said he needed various animal parts to cast spells.

Sudie Pearl, said Winfred's wife, was lucky to still be alive. Both neighbors swear they heard Hiram, after several family fights, tell Sudie Pearl "After I'm dead I'm going to dig my way out of the grave and come back and make you sorry you ever met me!" Other Toadsuck neighbors were really scared of old Hiram. He was constantly admiring someone's pet dog or cat and commenting on what specimens they would make in an experiment.

Folks did believe Hiram practiced black magic. And when pets started disappearing, Sheriff Otto Higgins got plenty of calls pointing the finger at Hiram. Sheriff Higgins told Dr. Bodkins at the pharmacy that at least two folks from Toadsuck had tried to collect a reward from the town's "Crime Stopper" program by reporting Hiram as the town's pet-napper.

When Hiram died suddenly, Sudie confided to one lady at the beauty shop that Hiram had, in the heat of one of their last marital discussions, again said that he hated her so much that when he died he was going to dig himself out of his grave and come back and make her wish she had never been born!

Well, Hiram's sudden and mysterious death caused tongues to wag. Several friends of the abused woman asked her, in light of Hiram's peculiar claim to black magic and the threats to dig himself out of the grave and come back and punish her, wasn't she afraid? Wasn't she somewhat worried?

"Naw," said Sudie Pearl. "Let him dig! I had him buried upside down!"

If You Haven't Found God, It Might Not Be Your Fault!

Although only eight and ten years old, the little Harvey boys, had already dealt their parents, Clemmie and Leon Harvey, enough misery with their mischief to last a lifetime. It seemed the boys were always getting into some kind of devilment, regardless of where they were. If any kind of mischief happened in Toadsuck and surrounding vicinity, the first people thought of as likely perpetrators were the Harvey boys.

It was just this type of reputation that brought a very frustrated Clemmie to the parsonage of Brother Titus Sistrunk. The pastor had proved to be a good disciplinarian of children within his own little flock. Perhaps his job at the State Reformatory, before his calling to preach, laid the groundwork for a successful record of straightening out boys who were considered incorrigible. And, while their mischief wasn't generally criminal in nature, the Harvey boys were at least borderline cases. If the boys could be jerked back in line, it would sure save Clemmie and Leon some frazzled nerves.

Pastor Sistrunk cheerfully invited Clemmie into his study to listen to her problems as she wrung out handkerchief after tear-soaked handkerchief while pouring out a seemingly unending list of less-than-civilized acts committed without remorse by the two young Harvey boys. Some were mere pranks, while others were costly to both the victim and to Leon when the boy's mischief resulted in retribution. Regardless, the folks in Toadsuck were glad that Clemmie was taking steps to bring the boys under control.

Pastor Sistrunk said he would like to talk to the boys individually. So Clemmi arranged for the eight-year-old to see the clergyman one Friday morning while the ten-year-old was busy helping his dad at the family's bait shop. The smaller of the boys timidly walked into the parsonage on Mayhaw Street and was greeted by Brother Sistrunk, who was a large man with a booming voice. He sat the boy in front of him and, looking him squarely in the eyes, asked in an authoritative voice, "Where is God?" The smaller of the town terrors looked shocked at the stern question but offered no reply.

The clergyman, still staring holes in the boy with his piercing eyes, repeated the question. This time a little sterner and in an unmistakably no-nonsense voice. "Where's God? I asked!" Again the littlest Harvey boy gave no response. Brother Sistrunk raised his voice and this time shook his pudgy finger in the boy's face. "WHERE IS GOD?" he boomed, verbally skinning the hide from the Harvey boy without laying a hand on him!

With this, the boy screamed and bolted from the pastor's study and ran home. He was breathless when he ran into the house and flung himself in the closet, pulling the door to behind him! By this time, his older brother was home from his morning's work and awaited his afternoon appointment with Pastor

Sistrunk. Hearing the ruckus in his brother's room he went in and seeing the closet door slightly ajar, jerked it open to find his little brother cowering in the darkness. "What happened?" he asked his trembling brother.

"Boy are we in deep trouble, Dude!" exclaimed the younger Harvey boy. "God's gone, and they think we done it!"

Just What the Doctor Ordered

The folks in Toadsuck were not the kind of people to take an interest in such foolishness as golf! Few if any had ever heard of the game, much less toted a bag of clubs around a cow pasture for the privilege of hitting a little white ball as far as they could, and then trudging over rocks and stumps until they found the ball, and then hitting it again as far as they could.

One Toadsucker, Homer Dingle, did get exposed to what he called "the foolish game of playing tag with the little white ball," when he visited a distant cousin who had moved to Fort Worth, where he had become a successful dirt-sucker salesman for the Hoover Company. The cousin said he found the golf links a favorable atmosphere for introducing new clients to the marvels of the Hoover, as most golfers have carpet in their homes. "Besides," said the cousin "I get plenty of fresh air and much needed exercise."

Homer's doctor had recently said that Homer should not consider his days sitting at the domino table in the Toadsuck Domino Palace as a stimulating sport, and he should find an outside activity other than digging for fishing worms for much needed exercise. Homer's run-down condition had been a worry to the usually cheerful brother of the manager of the town's sanitation department.

It took only one round on the Fort Worth golf course for Homer to find the answer to his doctor's orders. Fresh air and exercise were as much a part of this game of golf as were the little tin cups with the colored flags stuck in them, he discovered. Upon returning home, Homer couldn't wait to reveal his new-found healthy sport to his doctor.

The doctor was most impressed with this unusual display of upper class pastime activity discovered by one of Toadsuck's best known citizens. The doc suggested that Homer need not go all the way to Fort Worth to enjoy the healthy sport of golf. "Folks in the larger, nearby town of Denison have been playing golf for several years. Maybe Jim Bob Denby can drop you off there when he's taking over a load of pullets to the poultry processing plant."

Jim Bob, surprised at the request, was glad to drop Homer off at the Denison Municipal Golf Course on Avenue A. Homer became a regular rider to the golf course, where he could rent clubs at a nominal price. But the cost for his newfound sport was of no consequence to Homer as his improved health was well worth the expense of a day on the links.

One day at the golf course a member of the foursome that had invited the fellow from Toadsuck to join them had caught Homer nudging his ball out of the rough for a better shot. The man asked Homer, "Why do you cheat?"

Homer did not seem to be embarrassed by being caught cheating. Matter-of-factly the visitor from Toadsuck replied, "I play golf for my health, and winning makes me feel good!"

Old Ain't No Substitute for Books!

Lonnie Ray Culpepper, like most boys who haven't started to school yet, loved to visit his Grandpa Brumley who lived on a small farm just outside Toadsuck on FM 2152. Lonnie Ray, as could be expected, was inquisitive and just knew that Grandpa Brumley had lived long enough to know just about everything! And even better, the old man patiently listened to his myriad of questions without yelling one time, like his father did, especially when his dad was fishing. About all he got in the way of a response to his questions on their last fishing trip together was "SHHHH, you're skeerin' the fish!" So a visit to Grandpa Brumley's in Toadsuck would be the answer to an inquisitive boy's prayer. Lonnie Ray knew there would be no "SHHHs" from his Grandpa Brumley.

As was anticipated, Grandpa Brumley suggested the two take their usual walk in the nearby woods. They had barely cleared the front porch when the little tyke's barrage of youthful questions began. "Grandpa Brumley, how do birds know which way is south when it's time to migrate?"

"That has always been a puzzlement to me, too, Lonnie Ray, wish I could tell you," replied the boy's grandfather.

"Well, then," continued the boy barely missing a step, "where does the sun go when it sets?"

"Just don't know," said Grandpa Brumley, "maybe they'll teach you that when you start to school. If they do, will you be sure and tell me?"

"Well, Grandpa," asked Lonnie Ray, "are there really guardian angels, like Mommie says?"

"I 'spect there are, but I really can't say," answered the old man weakly.

Changing to a more earthly subject, Lonnie Ray asked his grandpa, "How do squirrels remember where they hide their acorns?" This being a rural question, Lonnie Ray was certain his grandpa from rural Toadsuck could give him an answer.

"Well boy, that is a question I asked my grandfather when I was about your age and he couldn't rightly say. Guess we will both have to wonder together." About this time, the pair reached Grandpa Brumley's front gate. Both were pretty exhausted not only from the long walk together, but also the exploration of all of Lonnie Ray's questions.

Seeing how tired the old man was, Lonnie Ray looked the old man in the eyes and said, "Grandpa, I'm sorry I asked so many questions today."

The kindly old man patted his visiting grandson on the head and said, "Lonnie Ray, never worry about asking your grandpa too many questions. After all, how is a boy going to learn if he don't ask questions?"

Growing Up in Toadsuck

Those who grew up in the little out-of-the-way community of Toadsuck, especially before the coming of the T&P Railroad and the town's subsequent absorption by the new railroad town of Collinsville, did so with a philosophy seemingly based on simplicity. Not that the people were incapable of complications, but all came from stock that had a preference for the simple, secure lifestyle. This was apparently passed on to their children. To the credit of folks from Toadsuck, they grew up lacking the distrust of their fellow man that more cynical big city residents had.

One example of their simplistic acceptance of one another was told by Agnes Tabor of Denison, about her eight-year-old grand-daughter, who came over from Toadsuck to spend the summer with her. The girl asked "Can I go outside and play with the boys?"

"No, you can't play with the boys, they're too rough," said the protective grandmother.

To this the little girl from Toadsuck, brought up to believe there is something good to be found in everyone, said, "If I can find a smooth one can I play with him?"

It stands to reason that not all kids growing up in Toadsuck developed at the same rate. When one four-year-old had not yet broken the habit of thumb sucking, his mother tried everything from bribery to reasoning. As a last resort she turned to threats. "If you don't stop sucking your thumb, your stomach will blow up like a balloon."

That afternoon the little boy saw a pregnant woman in the A&P. The four-year-old eyed her a few minutes and then, without batting an eye, walked up to her and said, "I know what you've been doing!"

A Little Knowledge Can Be a Dangerous Thing

Everyone was proud of Toadsuck's Elrod Dennerd, who was, so it seemed, to be the town's first collage graduate. But that was before the transgression that almost cost him his life and forever branded him, both in Toadsuck and at Texas A&M University, as "Engineering's loose cannon of the year." Elrod's plight started as an innocent college dormitory prank and escalated into one of Brazos County's most publicized crimes of the year.

It seems that Elrod and two of his cadet friends decided it would be great fun and and would heighten the rivalry between his school and the University of Texas if someone would steal a steer from a local rancher and haul it to Austin and substitute it for that school's famous mascot, Bevo. Their plan was to unmask the phony Bevo at A&M's next football game with UT. They could all have their laughs at the expense of their Austin rival and then return the purloined steer to its rightful owner.

Once a herd, from which the bogus Bevo would be taken, was located on the outskirts of College Station, the trio of high-spirited Aggies, led by Toadsuck's pride and joy Elrod Dennerd, drove to the ranch armed with a photo of the UT mascot, in a borrowed Chevrolet pickup. There, after looking over the herd in an attempt to steernap the animal that most favored the UT mascot, they found it difficult to decide which steer to "borrow" for the college practical joke. "To be on the safe side," suggested Elrod, "let's take two of the steers most likely to pass as Bevo."

The Aggies were able to entice the two purloined steers into the Chevy with a bale of coastal Bermuda grass brought along for just such an occasion. Feeling pretty proud of themselves and with great expectation of the switch that would prove to be a real conquest for A&M, the three high spirited young men, with their engineering leader at the wheel, drove from the pasture en route to Austin. As luck would have it Toadsuck's favorite son lead-footed it right through a red light not three-quarters of a mile from the U.T. campus. The black and white car that they almost dissected was not, unfortunately, a taxicab. It was Sergeant J. C. Crandall of the Texas Highway Patrol, who was stationed across the street and was on his way to the nearby Crispy Cream Do-Nut Shoppe for his morning sweet fix!

Within a matter of an hour Elrod and his two accomplices were standing in front of a justice of the peace, being arraigned for cattle rustling. All the explaining and elegant foot work in the world failed to sway the jury made up of ranchers from the Brazos County region, none of whom attended A&M.

The *Toadsuck Sentinel*'s announcement that their hope for having a college graduate was, along with the other two rustlers, convicted and sentenced to hang in Bryan on July 16, "After which a fried chicken basket lunch would be served by the Bryan Jaycees," was received with sadness and taken as an educational failure!

But educational failure it was not, for Elrod, on the day of the legal necktie party, proved his engineering education had not fallen on deaf ears. After the three cattle thieves were escorted up the steps of the freshly built gallows, they each took their place on the trap door that would permit them to drop suddenly to eternity! Sheriff Dusty Bledsoe gave the signal, and the hangman threw the lever that controlled the first trap door. A collective sigh went up as the trap door failed to open. The attending chaplain held his hand up for silence and said, "It appears that Almighty God does not wish this prisoner's life be taken." With that the sheriff commanded the young man to be released.

Moving to the second trap door, the hangman once again threw the lever. And once again, the trap door remained in place supporting the second young man. Again the county chaplain made the solemn pronouncement that God had, in his own way, spoken and the life of the second convicted rustler was not to be taken. Sheriff Bledsoe motioned for his deputy to release the second college student.

Becoming restless, and hungry for the promised fried chicken, the crowd that still remained stirred anxiously as Toadsuck's Elrod Dennerd's turn came. The Engineering student's brief life flashed across his mind as the sheriff signaled for the lever to be thrown for the third time. Once again, the trap door remained stationary. At this time Toadsuck's contribution to the Engineering profession looked at the hung trap door beneath his feet. After a moment he looked over and studied the lever that should have sprung the door. Once again the good chaplain held up his hand for quiet. When everything was still, Elrod, in a booming voice, said, "Sheriff, I think I see what the problem is!"

Hats Off to Friendliness

Had I not heard it directly from Harold Shanks, himself, I would not repeat it without reliable confirmation. Harold, a deacon in Toadsuck's Bethel Baptist Church, was not one with a reputation for gossip, exaggeration, and certainly not lying. Texans, having earned a reputation as "the friendliest people in

America," and folks in and around Toadsuck being the hand-shakingest folks in North Texas, is what makes the story so hard to believe. Shaking hands seemed to be a Toadsuck trait of long standing. On Saturday, when most folks in Toadsuck came to town, greeting one another made Main Street look like a Texas oil field full of pump jacks!

Harold told how one Sunday morning a stranger strode into the sanctuary just after the pastor had given the opening prayer. The man was wearing the biggest Stetson hat Brother Shanks had ever seen. He proceeded down the aisle and took a seat right in front of Pearl and Justin Kombeck. The man, Harold noticed, did not remove the big cowboy hat. Dumfounded at his lack of courtesy and respect, Harold, being a deacon, walked down the aisle and tapped the man on the shoulder. When the man looked up Harold pointed toward his Stetson. Unmoved by the gesture, the man still didn't take his hat off. The Kombecks as well as others were obviously peeved by the obstruction.

Harold told me he then leaned over to the stranger and whispered, "Will you please remove your hat in the church?" This time the man complied. And here is where the story strains credulity. When the service was over Harold took his place in the foyer at the top of the same aisle, where he waited as usual to shake hands with the worshipers as they left.

One of the last to depart was the stranger, still carrying the Stetson he had held in his lap throughout the service. As Harold stuck out his hand to introduce himself and welcome the stranger, the man, with a sheepish look, apologized for his conduct. "You see," he said, "I've been coming here for six months and not a soul has spoken to me. I decided I had to do something to get someone to speak to me!"

Being a Hero Can Be Costly

R. C. (Buck) Buchannan hadn't planned on becoming a Toadsuck celebrity that cold evening in October when he started out on the 16-mile drive from his home in town to check on a newborn calf at his place just outside of the Dixie community. And he certainly hadn't expected his sudden elevation to celebrity status would be so costly. Usually a levelheaded fellow, Buck had permitted himself to get caught up in the hubbub that had been generated by a few folks who swore that a "creature" unknown to the Toadsuck area had been seen as well as heard by more than a handful of usually respected residents. The creature of unknown origin seemed to mostly manifest itself at night on FM 1903 about halfway between Buck s home and his destination this night.

The rumor first started in the Toadsuck High School among young couples who had made the farm road a favorite nighttime necking place. Although many commented that they were surprised that the young folks could be distracted from their serious necking by something so flimsy as a creature long enough to give detailed descriptions of it. But, regardless of their absorption in their puppy-love activities, several had given graphic reports of their creature sightings. The sightings always occurred, as did their necking parties, on nights that were so dark even the fireflies collided in midair. While the details of the creature's appearance varied, all reporting the phenomenon agreed on one point. Their attention was drawn to the "creepy, shiny-coated, thing clambering and slithering from branch to branch in a huge tree just off the highway" by the sound it made. The young folks, as if reading from a script, agreed that with the car windows rolled down, no doubt to keep them from steaming up, they were attracted to an eerie "screeching sound." "The sound," added one young man, "was somewhat akin to that made by a hurt wildcat, but much louder." The groaning, rasping, sound made one focus on the top of the big tree from which the screeching sound came.

These reports became so numerous, as the youngsters repeated them to their parents, who then kept the reports alive by telling neighbors, that several credible adults made the nighttime drive to evaluate the creature sightings.

"Hub" Hubbard, the RFD mail carrier in that area, whose reputation for veracity was without critic, told his domino partners at the Toadsuck domino parlor, "Skeptic as I was, I made a nocturnal visit to FM 1903 and while I did not see the reported creature, I heard it plain as day!" He too, confirmed that in the nighttime quiet the shrill screeching noise was indeed unnerving. "There was no moon the night I went and my car lights picked up no unidentifiable object."

Hub's report was so convincing that even the usually skeptical Caroline Harris, publisher of the *Toadsuck Sentinel* printed a lengthy account of the "Toadsuck Creature" which had half the town scared out of its collective wits. The "voice of Toadsuck" even passed the story to the Denison paper whose reprint resulted in more nighttime traffic in the rural area around Toadsuck than anyone could remember. One reporter from Fort Worth interviewed Toadsuck pharmacist Doc Bodkins about the creature. The no-nonsense pharmacist dismissed the scare as "So much night soil."

But back to Buck Buchannan. The city-swelling farmer happened to select a night with a full harvest moon for his trip to check on his newly arrived calf. As he topped a hill approaching Chase Moore's place, he was shaken out of a near sleep by a blood-curdling, rasping, screech that raised the hackles on his neck. He instinctively pulled his pickup to the shoulder of the road and rolled down the half open window of the truck's passenger side. Once again his teeth were set on edge by a half growl, half whine that, Buck said, made him cringe with anxiety.

"I admit, while I was not afraid, not having seen the source of this unsettling sound, I knew something was out there. And it was something the likeness of which I had never seen. I reached overhead behind me and retrieved my 12-gauge pump shotgun which I had loaded with double ought shotgun shells, as I had been harassed at the farm by a coyote of unusual size, and I intended to put this chicken-thief out of business!

"Just as I stepped from the cab of my truck, I was again startled by the high-pitched growling sound which I determined was coming from across the road on the Moore place. Feeling a bit foolish, I had just put my shotgun back in the rack when the bright moon reflected on a silver-white object moving in the top of one of Chase's big oak trees. I watched, spellbound, for just seconds as the creature, which had been described perfectly, appeared to move from one branch to another in the very top of the tree. I took my eyes and my attention off the creature just long enough to remove my shotgun from its rack once again. About the same time, the unnerving squeal caused me to refocus my attention on the shiny object in the treetops. I was just seconds away from closing the books on what had been Toadsuck's mysterious creature, and I knew it.

"Without a second thought, and, certainly, with no thought of notoriety, I pointed my double-barreled shotgun upward toward the shiny white object I saw reflecting in the moonlight. Pulling both triggers, the double-barreled weapon slammed against my shoulder like the kick of a Missouri mule!

"The results were instant! I heard limbs being shattered and what sounded like the sheet iron that covered my barn hitting the ground. I remember being surprised that there was not a whimper from what was sure to be a mortally wounded creature.

"Climbing down the bar ditch, I approached Mr. Moore's fence. Had anyone been there, I am sure that, even in the blackest of nights, they could have seen how red my face was."

There on the ground under the big oak tree lay three galvanized steel blades of Farmer Moore's windmill, which, before it was "killed" by Buck Buchannan, turned behind the big oak tree. Its blades reflected in the moonlight, and their turning gave the illusion of something moving through the tree. Had Chase Moore oiled the bearings of his windmill more often, its groaning would never have drawn attention to the "creature" slithering through the big tree. With two 12-gauge shotgun shells Buck Buchannan had been thrust into celebrity status as the man who brought to an end the "Toadsuck creature."

Having known Chase Moore for many years, Buck's embarrassing admission of guilt in the destruction of the windmill was not sufficient. He felt obliged to bring the windmill back to its condition before it became the "creature" of fame in Grayson County. Buck's cost for being thrust into the limelight was $162.95.

Buck did earn a special place in the hearts of the young folks of Toadsuck, as now they could return to their favorite lover's lane without fear of the return of the "creature."

"Doc" Bodkin's Famous Hiccup Remedy

Folks around Toadsuck considered Toadsuck pharmacist H. P. "Doc" Bodkins with the same respect they did a regular medical doctor. His training and years behind the pharmacy counter had given him an exposure to the ailments of the public and the treatments that usually worked. Although not a licensed physician, Doc Bodkins could pretty well diagnose a medical condition and draw upon his experience with the powders, pills, and elixirs tucked away in the drawers behind the pharmacy counter and come up with a concoction to ease the suffering of his customers.

Not all discomforts required a magical potion from Doc Bodkin's bag of medicinal tricks, as was found out by Buford Staley one Saturday evening in July. Buford ran breathlessly into Bodkin's pharmacy and almost in a state of panic asked Doc Bodkin if he had a remedy for the hiccups. "Sure do!" answered Toadsuck's long-time druggist. With that, Bodkins stepped behind the store's soda fountain and drew a glass of cold water. He then turned and threw the glass of water smack dab in the face of Buford Staley. The bewildered customer, after recovering from the shock of being drenched by cold water, stammered, "Why in the world did you do a thing like that?"

The good pharmacist calmly faced his customer and said, "You don't have the hiccups anymore do you?"

Buford, whose face was as red as an overheated tea kettle, looked at Doc Bodkin and, as calm as his temper would permit, replied, "Never did have the hiccups; my wife, Iva June, outside in the car has the hiccups something terrible!"

You Just Can't Hide From the Truth

Jesse and Noreen Gage had been courtin' seriously ever since Jesse was big enough to drive a team of horses and hitch up his dad's hack. I guess the whole community around Toadsuck took for granted that the couple would eventually get hitched. They sure didn't try to hide their affection for one another. About the only part of the courtship that Jesse was a'skeerd of was having to face Noreen's pa, who was a grizzly-looking old codger who had raised Noreen alone since her ma died of the fever a few years after they came to Toadsuck from Tennessee.

The old man had, Jesse admitted, never been anything but nice to him, but just having to "beard the lion in his den" was Jesse's worst fear. The old man made a living from his few acres of sandy-land watermelons and from the paltry sum paid to him each year by Montgomery Ward in Fort Worth for the hides he tanned after running his traps. Perhaps a part of Jesse's fear came from the old man's smell after tanning his precious hides each day. After all, this primitive way of making a living was not without a lingering odor of decaying flesh mixed with chemicals. And bathing apparently was not the old man's long suit! But, Jesse knew the time was fast approaching when a face to face showdown would be required, as young folks in the early days of Toadsuck just didn't get married without the consent and blessing of the bride-to-be's father. And that was that!

So, as Noreen subtly applied the heat, Jesse began to brace for the formal occasion of his "asking for her hand," as it was called. Early one fall morning, when Jesse was sure the old man had finished the important job of running his traps, he hitched up the hack and started on the trek he had so often made, the drive to Noreen's place. The horses knew the route by heart. When he arrived he found old man Gage doing just what he expected he would be doing, stretching hides and hanging them to cure in the smokehouse. Jesse summoned up all the courage he could muster and called to Papa Gage through the smokehouse door.

"Come on in, Jesse, I been about halfway expecting you, the way Noreen has been mopin' around with her head in the clouds," said Mr. Gage, who was never one to pull any punches. Once inside Mr. Gage's workplace, Jesse surprised himself at how relaxed it flowed out of his mouth. "I come to ask you for Noreen's hand in marriage, Mr. Gage."

Noreen's Pa, who was left with four girls when his wife died, knew exactly why Jesse was sweating bullets as he stood there in the smokehouse among the family's cured hams, sausages, and the hides waiting to be shipped to Montgomery Wards. He knew it wasn't the temperature. After all, he, himself, had gone through the same time honored ritual when he and Noreen's ma got married.

Mr. Gage, in an effort to ease his soon-to-be son-in-law's tension, stoically looked Jesse over and let his eyes gradually come to rest on the recently stretched hides hanging from the smokehouse wall. Patiently and somewhat apprehensively Jesse waited for the old man's answer. Finally, after what, to the young suitor, seemed like an eternity, old man Gage, with a wry smile creasing his face, looked Jesse squarely in the eyes and said, "Jesse, I'm a little disappointed in you. You always struck me as an intelligent, discriminating young man."

Once again Noreen's pa let his eyes shift to the multitude of hides hanging in the smokehouse. "And now, of all the hides I have, you ask for the sorriest hide I got!" It was only then that Mr. Gage broke into an honest laugh, stuck out his hand, and welcomed Jesse into the family. Old man Gage sure had a way with making things easy, Jesse thought.

The Day Judgement Day Came to Toadsuck

Anyone who has been in Toadsuck for at least ten years still delights in telling newcomers about the time "Judgement Day" came to Toadsuck. One really needs to know the area around the community to get the full effect of this most momentous occasion.

The old Toadsuck cemetery is located on the Old Dixie Road about a mile and a half south of Toadsuck. Just inside the wrought iron fence on the east corner of the old cemetery is just about the largest native pecan tree in the region. It has produced pecans for more pecan pies and homemade candies than anyone can count. In November, right after the first frost has caused the hulls to turn loose of their nuts, local folks can be seen in the shade of the big old tree gathering nuts for the coming holiday baking.

One particular season, Willis and Junior Philpotts, whose place is about a quarter mile from the cemetery, went early to the nut tree to try to beat the Toadsuck city folks who were sure to scour the ground clean in just days. The two brothers, armed with a gallon syrup bucket, took only minutes to fill the container with the tree's fruit. The Philpotts boys crawled beneath the fence to go into the cemetery to divide their pecans.

"One for you, one for me. One for you, one for me." The dividing went on for twenty or so minutes. Their bucket was so full, some of the pecans overflowed and rolled back out under the fence. A neighbor boy, Claude Chastine, rode by on his bicycle. As he passed by he thought he heard voices in the cemetery. Stopping his bike he cupped his ears and listened intently. "One for you, one for me." Sure enough he did hear voices.

"Oh my!" he exclaimed, "Satan and St. Peter are dividing up the souls in the cemetery." Claude shuddered as he listened further, "One for you, one for me." About this time Claude saw old man Ezra Douglas hobbling down the Dixie Road. "Come here quick, Mr. Douglas, you won't believe what I heard. Satan and St. Peter are in the cemetery dividing up the souls."

"Shooo, you brat, can't you see with my lumbago I can hardly hobble home from here, much less hurry to take part in some Tomfoolery kid's game!" But after Claude's repeated pleas, old Ezra, lumbago and all, hobbled over to the fence where Claude was hanging on with sweaty palms for dear life. "One for you, one for me. One for you, one for me," he heard plain as day.

"Boy," he said to Claude, "you've been telling me the truth. Let's get closer and see if we can see ol' Satan, hisself." Shivering with fear, the old man and his young companion grabbed a fencepost and hung on for dear life as they strained both eyes and ears in an effort to see old Satan in the flesh. Then the voices continued, "One for you, and one last one for me. Now let's get those nuts by the fence, and we'll be through."

They say old Ezra made it back to town ten minutes ahead of the boy.

Xx Marks the Spot

Tyree and Amanda (Mandy) Ezell were two of Toadsuck's few colored residents. They, like most of the other coloreds, lived in the small yellow houses with brown trim that were furnished to employees of the T&P Railroad. Tyree preferred this "city living" to life on the few acres of farmland where his parents had lived when he was born. "Spending a lifetime looking at a mule's hind end, attempting to coax a bale of cotton out of the black gumbo soil of North Texas with a stubborn mule and a Blue Kelly plow just ain't appealing to a man with a mind for progress!" It was for this reason that Tyree went to work for the Texas and Pacific when they put the railroad northward around Toadsuck.

Not only did they furnish workers with a house, but it gave Tyree a chance to meet one of the ladies of color imported by the railroad to manage the cook shack and company laundry. It was at the cook shack that this Grayson County boy first laid eyes on Mandy.

Being perfectly happy in their little brown-trimmed yellow company house, Tyree and Mandy decided to sell off part of the remaining acreage at the old family farm. The county clerk drew up the necessary papers when Tyree had located a buyer. When the clerk presented Tyree with the deed to sign, Tyree made a big X and a little bitty x on the signature line. A bit puzzled, the clerk said to Tyree, "I can understand, not being able to read nor write, that the big X is your signature, but I don't understand why you added a little x after it."

"Well you see," said Tyree, "I bees a junior."

Lawyer's Funeral Bill Reveals More Than Prices

Toadsuck was still wet behind the ears when Fort Worth lawyer Calhoun Cotter hung up his shingle next to the Toadsuck Drugstore. Lawyer Calhoun practiced little criminal law. He spent much of his day probating wills and helping his clients secure clear titles on newly bought land. "Lawyer Calhoun," as he was known, was seemingly well liked by his clients and fellow townspeople. But he was still a lawyer. And as is the case nearly 100 years later, lawyers, while an admitted necessity, were still looked on with suspicion.

Lawyers in the last decade of the twentieth century were the butt of many jokes. During research of the folks who lived in Toadsuck, we found proof that this aversion to those who practice law by today's Texans is not of recent origin. When Lawyer Calhoun passed away in 1926, Percy Krum, who was Toadsuck's undertaker at the time, made a detailed accounting of the lawyer's funeral expenses. We noticed that there was a charge of $4 for gravediggers. We found that amount higher than was charged for the same service in the same time period. We asked Mr. Krum why Lawyer Calhoun had to pay more than other clients for the same service.

"It cost more to bury 'Lawyer Calhoun' than it cost to dig the average grave."

"Why did it cost more?" I asked.

His answer revealed much about the attitude of early Texans toward men who practiced before the bar of justice. "The average grave is five feet deep. We make it a practice of burying lawyers twelve feet in the ground, because we know down deep, they're really nice people."

Parenthetically Speaking

"Wickets" Wanslow was cruelly given his nickname in the fifth grade because his badly bowed legs reminded the kids of croquet wickets. After reaching manhood his parenthesis-like legs seldom were mentioned. That was until one day while filling in for an ailing clerk at Doc Bodkin's drugstore.

Millie Montgomery, who had little to brag about as for looks, dragged her overweight body into Bodkin's while Wickets was on duty. In today's jargon, Millie would be a poster girl for "thunder thighs." The flab on that woman's body would have kept a reducing salon in business a decade. Millie walked laboriously up to Wickets and asked him where the talcum powder was located. In an effort to help the dear lady find the product, Wickets said, "Walk this way."

Her reply cut Wickets to the quick. "If I could walk that way, Mr. Wanslow, I wouldn't need the talcum powder!"

Higher Education in Toadsuck

Almost from its beginning, Toadsuck recognized the need for a school system. Although not always the brightest of Grayson County's youngsters, the students left behind some memorable moments in Toadsuck's classrooms. A couple of these were told to me by early Toadsuck teacher Leroy Feeney. Mr. Feeney, now a bus driver for Mooney Touring Company, told how, in an effort to dramatize the dangers of exposing one's self to strong drink, Edger Peabody, a devout Baptist who taught biology at the Toadsuck school, scheduled a demonstration before his class which was to become one of the teaching profession's greatest embarrassments.

Mr. Peabody sat a drinking glass on his desk directly in front of the third period biology class. Into the glass he poured clear, pure water. From a small paper sack he produced two very much alive earthworms. Holding the glass high for all to see, Peabody dropped one of the squirmy creatures into the glass of water. The class watched in rapt attention as the worm wriggled happily on the bottom of the glass of water.

Mr. Peabody then produced a pint bottle of whiskey borrowed for this occasion. After emptying the water from the glass and placing the lively worm back into his sack, the teacher poured the whiskey into the glass. The amber fluid was clear enough that the bottom of the glass could be easily seen. He then produced the second worm scheduled to prove his point about the evils and dangers of alcohol consumption.

The class of eager, young minds watched open-mouthed as Peabody dropped the lively worm into the glass containing the whiskey. They watched in horror as the poor creature began to change from a glowing red to a dingy brown, and to shrivel up into a knot! Within seconds the once active earthworm was obviously dead. His, they thought, must have been a horrific tormented death! Mr. Peabody had, through his masterful demonstration, made his undying point. Or had he?

After the children had settled into a quiet, more reflective frame of mind, their teacher, quite proud of the lesson he had left on their impressive minds, called on one of the class' brightest students, Tyrone Philpots, who lived just outside Toadsuck on a farm. "Now Tyrone, what did you learn from our dramatic experiment?"

Tyrone, never a shy one, spoke up in a firm, positive voice. "Mr. Peabody, the way I see it, if you drink whiskey you won't have worms!" While the class was tittering at Tyrone's lesson-killing explanation, Mr. Peabody quietly packed his pint of whiskey into the paper sack containing the first, very much alive earthworm and left the room with a blistering red face.

Another less than effective teaching experience in the Toadsuck school was told to me by Lucinda Blevens, who attended the Toadsuck school before her family moved to South Texas. Mr. Blevens was to take a job putting out smoke pots in the citrus orchards of the Rio Grande Valley in the event of an unseasonably cold winter. Although only a sporadic job, it was a step up from Mr. Blevens' current position as signal light maintenance man in a town with only one signal light!

Lucinda was a classmate of Lonnie Ray Perkins in Miss Lottie Courtney's class. Lucinda said Miss Courtney, in a test of her psychology skills, started her class one day by saying, "Everyone who thinks they are stupid stand up." After a few seconds Lonnie Ray stood up. "Do you think you are stupid, Lonnie Ray?" asked Miss Courtney.

"No Ma'am," answered the tow-headed youngster, "but I hate to see you standing there all by yourself."

Who Said "Thin is Always Better"?

Although it didn't happen in Toadsuck, it won the "Champion Liars" contest's first prize for Jerry Bob Todd at Toadsuck's annual Men's Hunting and Fishing Club "Liars Night" banquet, to which the wives of the club members were always invited. Probably in an effort to pay back the women for all the time the men spent away from their families during the various hunting and fishing seasons. This masculine extravaganza featured dinner prepared by the menfolk and was topped off by awarding a prize, usually a new hunting jacket or fishing waders or some other item dedicated to keep the menfolk away from home even more. The prizes are donated by Lee Harvey's Bait and Tackle shop located on FM 1562. Last year's prize was a gift certificate for a choice of ten dozen minnows or night crawlers.

Although most of the lies told by the members were hunting and fishing lies, Jerry Bob's whopper came, he said, from a Fort Worth newspaper. "And," said Jerry Bob, "reflects how low true love has sunk."

He said a Fort Worth lady was in the midst of a shower when she heard a knock at her door. According to Jerry Bob the lady yelled, "I'm in the shower, who is it?" To this came the reply, "It's the police, your husband has been run over by a steam roller!" Upon hearing this, the woman responded, "Just slide him under the door, I'll be out in a minute!"

"It's just relationships such as this that causes men to go hunting and fishing so often," added a daring Jerry Bob, to the amusement of the men only.

The Miracle Machine

With the two-story Masonic Lodge and Eastern Star building being the tallest structure to grace the Toadsuck skyline, it is easy to see why "Boots" Swink reacted the way he did the first time he saw an elevator.

It was not just dumb luck that made it possible for Boots and Nettie Mae Swink to take their son, Harley, on a weekend trip to Fort Worth at the expense of the Toadsuck Co-Op Cotton Gin.

Boots and Nettie Mae both had toiled from rooster crow till sundown all season trying to produce Toadsuck's first bale of cotton for the year. The gin had always rewarded the producer of the first bale with a weekend trip to the big cotton auction in Fort Worth. Harley, though only ten years old, had done his part to bring home this enviable honor! Boots' only hesitation in accepting the coveted prize was Nettie Mae.

Speaking of prizes, Nettie Mae was not one. She was a hatchet-faced, "tall, skinny drink of water," as folks called her. Her chest was flat as a fritter, and her daily exposure to the scalding Texas sun as she hoed Johnson grass from the cotton rows and tended her small garden of collard greens and poke salet had left her skin a mite shriveled up. Boots always said, "If Nettie Mae didn't have an Adam's apple, she wouldn't have a figure at all." Her shape made dressing her up difficult even for the Sears and Roebuck catalog. But, despite her looks, Nettie Mae Swink, clutching Harley's hand, found herself boarding the T&P for Fort Worth for their hard-fought-for weekend.

The height of the weekend was Boots' visit to the Fort Worth Cotton Exchange Building where he would get to see his bale of cotton go on the auction block. But, as things turned out, this event, thrilling as it was, would not be the highlight of Boots' trip. No Siree, Bob!

On the morning of the auction, Boots and Harley made their way to the tall Cotton Exchange Building on West Seventh Street. As they stepped into the lobby of the tall building, the father and son found themselves facing a shiny, stainless steel wall. As they straightened their slightly wind-blown hair in the reflection of the shiny steel wall, to their surprise, the wall parted, revealing a small room in front of them. Standing next to Boots facing the little room was a middle-aged man and a woman whom Boots thought to himself was even uglier than his Nettie Mae. This woman was fat and had face wrinkles like a woman twice her age should have. The little crinkles around her mouth were stained brown from collecting years of snuff. She had crow's feet that made her eyes look like bulging prunes! Her sack-like dress made her look like twenty pounds of flour in a ten-pound sack!

To Boots' surprise, as the stainless steel wall opened, the couple stepped into the little room. The wall then went back together and Boots and Harley watched as the hand on the clock above the opening in the wall started to move. The clock hand stopped on the number six and then after a pause, started to return to number one again. The stainless steel wall opened again and to Boots' surprise, out stepped the man who had stepped in only a few minutes earlier. But instead of the flour sack-looking woman who had gone into the little room with the man, he was with a shapely, voluptuous, blond lady in a fashionable dress and tiny, tiny shoes. Her face was particularly fetching. She had ruby red lips and a powdered nose like Boots had seen in the nickelodeon films in Denison.

It was hard for him to comprehend this astounding miracle he had witnessed! He immediately turned to Harley and said, "Son, run back to the hotel and get your mama!"

Young Love is Undying

Nita Barlow had no intentions of prying into the personal life of her sixteen-year-old daughter, Cassie, when she discovered and read a letter Cassie had received from her steady boyfriend, "Slick" Sly. Cassie had neglectfully left the folded letter tucked under her pillow. When Cassie found the letter while making Cassie's bed, she, as a woman, was tempted to quietly throw it away. It was, she thought, a little like someone reading her diary when she was a girl. But, as a mother, she thought it her duty to know exactly the seriousness of her daughter's relationship with Slick.

If this letter was any indication of the Sly boy's romantic intentions toward her daughter, she felt there was little to worry about, at least at this time. Her husband, Cleon, would be glad to know that there was little chance of an immediate elopement. The letter read as follows:

"Dear Cassie, My love for you grows with each moment. When we are next to each other in class I can hardly contain myself. I know now my love knows no bounds! There is nothing strong enough to keep us apart. I would fight anyone to defend your honor. Even "Bulldog" Crumby. Nothing has been created that is powerful enough to restrain me from being with you, my true love! Toadsuck has never seen a love as limitless as mine for you. And don't forget, I'll pick you up to take you to the dance over at Dixie next Tuesday, if it don't rain. Yours forever, Slick."

One Man's Opinion!

Folks in Toadsuck always looked forward to receiving their weekly *Toadsuck Sentinel*. One could always count on there being something new in it. "That," said its editor, Caroline Harris, "is precisely why it is called a newspaper!" Even Caroline had to admit while it wasn't exactly the *New York Times*, it still could be counted on to bring the reader something that they wouldn't get anywhere else.

Like yesterday's issue, for example, I could hardly believe my eyes, yet there it was in black and white! It was right there pointed out in a neat little black bordered box, which I am sure Caroline charged extra for. An ad that gave me such a laugh it should have been in the funnies, if the *Sentinel* had a funny paper! The ad read as follows:

Lost—Dog with three legs, blind in left eye, missing right ear, broken tail, accidentally neutered. Answers to name of "Lucky."

This ad is likely to pay off for the advertiser as "Lucky" should be easily spotted. Like I said, it is items like this that makes subscribing to the *Toadsuck Sentinel* worthwhile!

A Grave Misunderstanding!

Leroy Dennerd, so it seemed, could never hold down a job, even in the best of times in Toadsuck. No one knew if it was his personality that resulted in his changing jobs with the waxing and waning of the moon, or if he was really inept in everything he tried.

He was the only one in Toadsuck's history who ever lost his job as a milker at the Toadsuck Dairy because of cold hands. We know the cows couldn't blow the whistle on Leroy, so how, you ask, do we know he had cold hands?

When Leroy's production began to slide, "Dutch" Schindler, who managed the dairy for the Culver Brothers, the dairy owners, got to watching Leroy on the job. He noticed that as the cows lined up to go into the milking stalls, they seemed to intentionally shy away from the stall where Leroy sat with his bucket. Surprised is not the word for how Dutch felt about the cow's seemingly organized strike against Leroy.

Whatever the reason, those cows scheduled to feel the hands of Leroy Dennerd shunned his touch like he had the plague. As a result, Leroy's production declined so much it was decided he had to be replaced. It fell on Dutch to break the news to the oft-unemployed worker. Dutch couldn't allow his like for the good old boy to stand in the way of making room for a milker who could increase production at the town's only dairy. This was especially true since two new delivery routes had been started in the Greasewood-Cottondale community. A man with a good grip and plenty of pull was needed to meet the demand of the dairy's new customers.

Dutch went down to the milking barn to break the news to Leroy. He arrived just as the morning milking was about to begin. Sure enough, as he approached Leroy's regular milking stall, he watched in amazement as old Bossy, one of the dairy's highest producers, took a look at Leroy and made a quick turn in the direction of the gate that leads out to the farm's green pasture.

"Then," Dutch related later, "the next cow, as if guided by some bovine radar, looked up and saw Leroy in the stall awaiting his next

victim. The ol' gal switched her tail a couple of times and, I'll swear, made a bee-line in the direction of the gate to the pasture. The cows seemed to have made a pact to avoid Leroy. It was then I made up my mind that firing Leroy was inevitable.

"I walked slowly up to the stall and stuck out my hand, wanting to part company on friendly terms. This handshake was to prove most revealing. Leroy's hands," Dutch continued, "were like icebergs. My first thought was, If I were a cow, I wouldn't want Leroy's icy fingers coming near my tender parts. I never knew cows to strike," commented Dutch, "but sure as the cream rises to the top, our cows had gone on strike as far as Leroy was concerned!"

Word about Leroy's latest reentry into the job market came as no surprise to the menfolk in Toadsuck. What did shock them was Helen Dennerd's announcement a couple of weeks later that her husband was again employed. "This time," she proudly proclaimed, "Leroy has five hundred people under him!" Where in the world could Leroy be holding down such a job, they wondered, and justly so. There wasn't an employer with that many employees in Toadsuck, or in the entire county, come to think of it.

Then they found out that Leroy did have a job with five hundred people under him. He was the caretaker at the Toadsuck cemetery.

Getting Really High in Toadsuck

When Otis Campbell went on a toot, most anything could be expected. But no one ever thought of Otis ever being a space traveler. That was until Clif Pearson, Toadsuck's respected barber, ran into Otis one rainy night as the town's lush attempted to make his way home after a riotous evening of who-can-destroy-his-liver-first drinking with the boys. Clif tells the story much better than I, but in his absence, I'll do my best.

Clif said he came upon Otis as he stood on the corner of Mayhaw and Persimmon. Although it was late at night, the moon cast its silvery sheen on Toadsuck's wet street. Otis, said Clif, was standing on the corner with his eyes transfixed on a puddle of rainwater that had accumulated in the street by the curb. The moon's orb reflected brightly in the murky water. As Clif interrupted Otis' fixation on the puddle, the drunk pointed down and asked Clif, "What is that light down there?"

Clif replied, "That, Otis, is the moon." Otis drew himself up to his full height and in a quizzical tone of slurred speech said, "Moon! What the hell am I doing way up here?"

Take a Number

Jeremiah Dunlop, one of Toadsuck's early settlers, told a tale that still leaves a bad taste in some folks' mouths. Jeremiah, who was not prone to stretch the truth except, maybe, when caught in a tight spot himself, really had little reason to lie. Jeremiah said that he had only been in Toadsuck a few weeks when he saw the strangest funeral procession he had ever seen.

He said first came a man riding a mule with a black mourning blanket. Following the mule was a white funeral coach pulled by six matched white horses. This coach was followed by a second white funeral hearse drawn by an equal number of white horses. Behind the two coaches was a line of what Jeremiah estimated to be about twenty-five men.

Jeremiah couldn't bear not knowing about the strange sight. He said he ran to the man riding the mule and asked who had died. The man, according to Jeremiah, said that his mule, the very one he was riding, had kicked his wife in the head, killing her. She was in the first funeral coach. The man said his mother-in-law came to mourn his loss and she, too, had been fatally kicked by the mule. She was in the second funeral coach.

"Would you consider selling your mule?" asked Jeremiah.

"Get in line," answered the man, pointing to the line of men following the two hearses.

Reading Between the Lines!

Toadsuck, for the most part, was a friendly town. Few conflicts arose among the town's small population. The only one I can say I remember was the result of a totally unintentional misunderstanding between Rufus Satterwhite, who had a small farm just outside of town on the Dunlop Ferry Road near Pettibone Peach orchards, and a town dweller by the name of Freddy Jenkins.

Rufe put an ad in the *Toadsuck Sentinel* offering a horse for sale for $50. The Jenkins fellow called Rufe up and said he was interested in the horse but wanted to know why it was so cheap. Rufe, always a square shooter, told Mr. Jenkins the horse didn't look so good.

"I'll come out and take a look, and if I like him, I'll take him," said Freddy. Sure enough the Jenkins fellow made the drive out to the Satterwhite place to see the horse.

"If you take him and find him not as I have described him, I'll refund your money." Mr. Jenkins paid Rufe and led the animal into the trailer he had brought along. About three days later Mr. Jenkins called Rufe and wanted a refund on the horse. "This horse," he complained, "is almost totally blind."

"I can't take the horse back," said Rufe.

"But," whined Freddy, "you said if he was not as described you would refund my money."

"Yes," responded Rufe, "but didn't I tell you the horse didn't look so good?"

Although he felt taken, Mr. Jenkins didn't hold a grudge, realizing he had bought a powerful lesson in rural merchandising.

What's in a Name?

Plenty, if you happened to live in Toadsuck, Texas. Collinsville, the successor to the town of Toadsuck, on the KATY railroad line in southwestern Grayson County was named for early settler L. B. Collins. It is probably a good thing that the residents of Toadsuck were absorbed by the new town of Collinsville, not only because of the railroad, but for name identification! While there are few still around who can say what residents of Toadsuck were called, it's a sure bet that some laughingly referred to them as "Toadsuckers!"

Why Toadsuck's Fences Were Only Armpit High

Toadsuck's houses were generally surrounded by picket fences, all built to a uniform armpit height. They were built to this specification for the same reason most Toadsuck women who patronized Opal's Kurl Up and Dye Beauty Salon refused to sit under Opal's hair dryers. Try as hard as she might, Caroline Harris could never attract the interest in her weekly newspaper, the *Toadsuck Sentinel*, that was generated at the backyard fences and beauty shop chairs in the town. The reason was quite elementary. Most of the town's local news, at least the type most of the women could relate to, was disseminated by the picket fence media. Seeing a neighbor lady with arms hanging over one's backyard fence usually indicated that a choice bit of electrifying news was about to be exchanged.

This same bit of news might, not unlike the Associated or United Press wire services, be relayed by word of mouth from one beauty shop customer to another. Which is why no woman with an interest in keeping abreast of current events in Toadsuck would risk missing a piece of local news by being caught under a hair dryer while a tasty morsel was relayed from one customer to another!

Miss Harris had often said that her greatest fear was that Toadsuck's distaff population would develop a means of selling advertising of local goods and services to be inserted between the various items of "over-the-fence" news reports, which would eliminate the need for her weekly newspaper, except for the kids to use in making kites and for lining the bottoms of canary cages.

Rural Faux Pas

No woman in Toadsuck, especially those chosen few who are or have been members of that small society group known as the Toadsuck Garden Club, does not know the story of how Birdie Dinwitty lost her position as president of that elite organization. Birdie, while in a state of euphoria after being mentioned in the society column of the county's largest newspaper, *The Denison Voice of Reason*, volunteered to host the Garden Club's spring tea at her home next door to the Toadsuck Funeral Home. While a challenge, the event would give her some local recognition as a "society matron," which would long be remembered. Long remembered is right! But not exactly as she envisioned, thanks to the apple of her eye, her six-year-old daughter, Sunshine Dinwitty.

The morning of the much anticipated and talked about spring tea, Birdie woke up with a dilemma. She knew children of Sunshine's age were prone to take note of anything unusual, and she was aware that the guest list included Lucinda Breedlove, who, although one of Toadsuck's leading citizens, was endowed with a very large nose!

Birdie had once remarked that she had canned squash of the same size. Birdie was sure that any child, even a child as well brought up as her Sunshine, couldn't help but notice the famous Breedlove proboscis. Wanting to make sure that little Sunshine didn't embarrass her by staring at the Breedlove nose, Birdie decided to caution the darling girl before the guests arrived. Birdie called little Sunshine into the house hours before the guests were

scheduled to arrive. She then began her brief-
ing as to how the golden-haired child
should conduct herself.

"Darling, Mrs. Breedlove will be
among our guests today, and as you
know the nice lady has a very big
nose. I beg you to please make an effort not to stare at Mrs.
Breedlove's oversized nose." The child indicated that she would
do nothing to attract attention to the lady's large nose. Feeling
more confident after the little talk with Sunshine, Mrs. Dinwitty
went on with her preparation for the club's biggest event of the
year. She looked at the clock every fifteen minutes in anticipation
of the guests' arrival. She was hosting the cream of Toadsuck's
womanhood! All eyes would be on the Dinwitty house.

An hour before the guests were due to arrive, Birdie felt that
one more warning wouldn't hurt. After all, she thought, she's
only six years old. And one knows how flighty the minds of kids
are. After calling Sunshine in for a last look at her bright yellow
satin dress with a hair bow to match, the nervous hostess pulled
the little girl to her side. "Now remember our little talk about
Mrs. Breedlove's large nose! Whatever you do don't let yourself
stare at her nose."

"Yes, Mama," promised the pride of the Dinwitty household,
"I won't forget. I'd never do anything to embarrass you, Mama!"
Now, said Birdie to herself, I can relax and concentrate on the for-
malities of the tea.

One by one the guests arrived and were seated at the
Dinwitty's large round heirloom table with the family's silver
service polished to a high gloss sitting in the middle. Birdie, leaving nothing to chance with her Sunshine, sent the little doll into
the backyard to play until the tea was over. After a short meeting

of the Toadsuck Garden Club, time came for the hostess to serve tea. Making sure each member had her teacup and saucer, not to mention a silver demitasse spoon, Birdie, who was sure not to be forgotten following such an elaborate (for Toadsuck) social event, poured the tea herself.

When she came to Lucinda Breedlove, she politely asked, "Do you use sugar or cream in your nose?"

The following week, at the club's annual meeting, Birdie Dinwitty resigned her prestigious position, which also made the Denison society column.

A Kodak Moment at Silver Leaves Retirement Center

Seventy-eight-year-old Myra Pickett could not be held totally to blame for her shameful conduct on that warm spring day when she removed every stitch of clothing she was wearing and dashed around the Silver Leaves Retirement Center's veranda as fast as her walker would allow!

Myra had attended every session of Rhonda Schmidt's discussions on "Keeping young as you age." Hadn't the pretty activities coordinator said that "In order to keep youthful, one should put aside old ideas and try to focus on more trendy, current activities?" Just yesterday Myra was reading in a 1952 edition of the *Fort Worth Star-Telegram*, left behind by a Sunday visitor, where college students in Ohio were streaking stark naked around the basketball court during a game with a neighboring college. Now, if that isn't trendy and current, I don't know what is, thought the elderly resident.

Myra selected a time when the veranda was most crowded with residents and their visitors to act out her attempt at pursuing new, more youthful activities. Myra also knew that Benjamin Crowder, who ate at the table next to hers, always went out on the porch about two hours after the noon meal. Myra had caught old Ben staring at her on a couple of occasions. It had been a long time since any man had paid any attention to the aging resident.

Sure enough, Ben was sitting next to Elmer Daggett when Myra whizzed past the two sans clothing. Elmer was the first to speak after he recovered from the impromptu imitation of Sally Rand. "Wasn't that Myra Pickett?" he asked Ben.

"Sure was," replied Ben, still aghast. "Looks like she could have taken time to iron her dress before she came out where all the visitors are."

You Can Count on Your Family!

Ten-year-old Seth McGee, whose father was the pastor of a small church just outside of Toadsuck, approached his father after the family's Sunday dinner. "How high can you count?" asked young Seth.

"Don't rightly know, son," replied the preacher, "never really tested myself."

"Well," said Seth, beaming proudly, "I can count to seven thousand, five hundred and thirty-two."

"And," asked his father, "why did you stop there?"

"Because," answered his son, "your sermon was over."

Unsurpassed Comeuppance

Lonnie Ray Timpkins, despite his upbringing, had a way about him that seemed to grow trouble, somewhat like mushrooms grow in dank, dark places. Perhaps it was more his greediness than anything else that brought him into disfavor with others. He was the type of fellow who, when offered a second helping of pie, would always take one, even though others at the table hadn't yet been served. He seemed not to worry that there might not be enough pie to go around, and that the offer was more one of courtesy than anything else!

When the guys at the Toadsuck Domino Palace all chipped in to buy a round of soda pop from Bodkin's Drugstore, it was Lonnie Ray who was always a bit short of cash, but would ante up double next time. The other players at the table knew Lonnie would end up riding free, but they had rather foot the bill than argue over a half dollar.

Someone once commented that Lonnie must have had it really hard during the Depression, when it was a dog-eat-dog world. It was like he swore to himself that he would never do without again, regardless of who had to sacrifice to make him satisfied! This was especially true of anything to eat. But Lonnie Ray's chickens all came home to roost one Sunday afternoon when he went to the Autumn Leaves Nursing Home just on the outskirts of Toadsuck to see his mother.

Mrs. Timpkins, who was well up into her eighties, had been in the home ever since Mr. Timpkins passed

away. Mrs. Timpkins shared a room with another lady who was about the same age. It was Lonnie Ray's own mother who told the story of that fateful day when Toadsuck's most notorious freeloader got his comeuppance in spades. Although she hadn't meant it to go outside the nursing home, by telling Eula Greenleaf, who did her hair as a weekend volunteer in the home's small beauty shop, she might just as well have put it in Caroline Harris' weekly *Toadsuck Sentinel*. Mrs. Timpkins should have known that when Eula hit the front door at her regular job at Opal's Kurl Up and Dye Beauty Parlor, the story would be the "Have you heard" of the day!

Well, anyway, the cat was out of the bag, and when the wives of the town's domino players shared it at home, the husbands slapped their knees in approval. According to Lonnie Ray's mother, when Lonnie came for his weekend visit, her roommate was sound asleep. As Lonnie Ray brought his Mama up to date on all the latest news, he noticed a small glass bowl filled with Spanish peanuts sitting on the roommate's night table. Not wanting to disturb the sleeping woman, Lonnie Ray decided it would be all right to nibble on the peanuts. By the time his visit was almost over, the town "moocher" had nibbled the bowl empty.

Just as he was giving his mother a farewell kiss on the forehead, her roommate awoke from her Sunday nap. In a feeble attempt to make amends for taking advantage of her roommate, Lonnie Ray leaned over and in a most sincere tone of voice apologized for eating all the dear lady's peanuts. "I just started nibbling, and before I knew it they were gone," said Lonnie Ray.

"Don't fret none about it," said the roommate in a soft and kindly voice. "I had already sucked the chocolate off!"

The "Pecking Order" Was Never in Doubt at Odie Clanton's

When Odie Clanton took the job as short-order cook at the Toadsuck's Elite Eatery, it caused some raised eyebrows! The town's diner had always employed a woman in that very busy job. The menfolk especially expressed doubts as to a man's ability to perform up to par in the culinary department, even though it involved, at the most, the frying of a few eggs, most of which were well done. Most men don't tolerate hen-fruit with runny yokes! They say runny yokes tend to mix with their morning grits, which they hold sacred and demand they be hot and perfectly white to be palatable. "Yoke yellow in grits just aren't southern," they protested.

It took only about a week behind that greasy white apron for Odie to earn the acceptance of the diner's regular customers, but they still wondered why Odie was so efficient in what was usually, by the standards of Toadsuck, considered "woman's work." This was before they had seen Odie and his dear Corine together. It took the annual Grange pancake supper to open the eyes of the folks of Toadsuck, and to make the menfolk happy they had their wives instead of Odie's Corine.

Corine, who was well thought of in the Women's Auxiliary of the Grange, had volunteered to do one shift of pancake cooking at the Toadsuck chapter of the Grange's supper. What her peers didn't know was that the reason she volunteered for this hot, batter-spattering job was that she intended for Odie to do most of the cooking and the horrendous clean-up job afterwards, just as he did at home!

It seems that Odie's marriage was based on the kind-hearted, peace-loving man's dancing to whatever tune Corine sang! To say that Odie was henpecked was a disservice to the poultry world. There never was a chicken that expected as much of a rooster as Corine expected of Odie Clanton. Although he definitely wore the pants in the Clanton family, they could never be seen as they were constantly covered up with an apron! Odie later confided to Joe Bob Perkins that when they married, "Corine couldn't make ice tea without looking at the recipe."

The night of the long-awaited pancake supper, Corine was giving more orders than the paying customers. "But," confided Mavis Roundtree, "all of them were to Odie!" Mavis said at one time Odie was at the big grill making the fluffy flapjacks when Corine, seeing a few getting too brown, yelled at Odie, "Flip!"

"At this," swore Mavis, "Odie grabbed his knees and did the best backflip she had ever seen." Yes, when Corine said "Frog!" Odie jumped. If Mavis is to be believed, the "head" of the Clanton household was so henpecked and used to doing exactly as he was told, once, while visiting a Fort Worth store, he saw a sign that said, "WET FLOOR," so he did!

Look on the Bright Side!

Otis and Nelda Faye Potter's little girl, Sarah, was one of Toadsuck Elementary school's brightest students. Not in the educational sense of the word, but she had a way of making her teachers feel glad they had accepted the special calling a teacher needed to endure the trials related to the job. Sarah's smiling face and cheery words could be counted on to start each day, regardless of how bad the day before was. This same quality was just as visible at home. Although Otis lost his job one year at the

Toadsuck Ice and Fuel Company, Sarah did much to wipe away her mother's worries just by her cheerful attitude. Although it didn't bring in any much-needed income, at least hers was the only face in the Potter household that wasn't so long it swept the floor when she walked.

Normally Sarah, like other Toadsuck children, walked home from school each day. But today, Nelda Fay looked skyward at the ominous black clouds sagging by the water inside. She decided to drive to the little school and pick Sarah up so she wouldn't be soaked by the rain that was sure to come. This simple event served to point out Sarah's innocent, positive attitude that had so affected everyone to whom she was exposed!

Nelda Fay arrived at the school just as classes were dismissed. She turned just in time to see her daughter running in her direction. About that time a lightening bolt flashed. While many children of Sarah's age would be in tears, Nelda Faye saw Sarah look skyward and smile. The big smile that creased her face was easy for all to see. Sarah continued to run toward her mother's aging car. Nelda Faye flinched as another gigantic lightening bolt filled the sky with brilliant, but frightening, yellow light. She opened her tightly squinched eyes in time to see Sarah look to the heavens and again smile the biggest smile. This was repeated several times before the little girl climbed into the front seat of her mother's car. Nelda Faye immediately inquired as to the child's strange behavior. "Why, in all that rain, did you keep stopping and looking into the sky and smiling?" Nelda asked the little girl. The answer she got should not have surprised her, but it did!

"I had to, Mama. God was taking my picture."

The Brush Arbor

During the summer months, which could be scalding hot in Toadsuck, Texas, several of the churches held their annual revivals under brush arbors. A brush arbor is nothing more than a tent-like covering made by laying tree limbs and other brush across a frame constructed overhead. The Full Gospel Church was not the only one that used a brush arbor, but theirs seemed to draw the largest crowds. They seemed to always have two or three baptizings in Toadsuck Creek before the "dinner-on-the-grounds" that marked the end of their revival.

One of their frequent "hellfire and brimstone" preachers was ol' Brother Abner Watkins from Waco. He always was a crowd pleaser with his flare for the dramatic in his sermons. He was known to keep the mourner's bench full at nearly every service. The congregation included the Harvey family with their two rambunctious boys, Lee and Thedford. The boys persuaded Mr. Harvey to let them bring their pet possum with them on the last night of the revival, under the condition it be kept on its hemp leash. The boys swore an oath that the rural equivalent of a pet dog would remain tied under their bench during the service.

Prior to the last service, pastor Watkins had arranged with the church deacons to finish with a dramatic flourish. He asked them to push some of the brush away from the middle of the overhead arbor so that the starlit sky was exposed to those in attendance. During the last part of Brother Watkins' sermon, the Harvey boy's pet possum chewed through the small rope that bound him to their bench and escaped. As the preacher wound up his sermon he asked the congregation to "Join me in giving thanks for a glorious revival by lifting our eyes toward God's starry heaven and repeat after me. 'My God! What a rat!'"

An Innocent Misunderstood Sarcasm

Little Beulah Lee Potter, a bright pupil in Miss Pettybone's third grade class in the Toadsuck Elementary School, was most earnest when she answered her teacher's question on the last day of the school term before classes were dismissed for summer vacation. It was just a little shocking to the young teacher.

In preparing her charges for the carefree days ahead, Miss Pettybone told them, "You will be having a lot of happy times in the months ahead. I'd like for you to think of some of the happy things you will be doing and let's spend our last day in class having happy thoughts. I'm going to ask each of you to share with the class what you are going to do this summer that to you is a happy thought."

The teacher had barely taken her seat at the front of the class after giving the children the day's assignment when up went the hand of little Beulah Lee. "Alright, Beulah Lee, are you ready to tell the class what you are going to do this summer that is for you a happy thought?"

"Yes, Miss Pettybone, I think this summer I'm going to be pregnant." The teacher reeled at this shocking answer, to which several in the class tittered, although they didn't know why they were laughing. Once Miss Pettybone recovered her composure she faced the girl and asked her, "Now, Beulah Lee, what makes you think that is a happy thought?"

"Because my daddy is about the smartest person I know, and this morning at the breakfast table my mama said to him, "Eugene, I think I might be pregnant," and he said, "Now *that's* a happy thought!"

Toadsuck's Last Lawyer

When prominent Sherman lawyer Spencer Calhoun decided to move his practice to Toadsuck in hopes of picking up more rural Grayson County business, he bought a brand new auto in an effort to impress the locals. He flaunted his new Lincoln under the noses of his new Toadsuck neighbors.

He had only been in town a few days when he took the new car into "Waxey" Wilhite's Main Street Car Wash to get it all shiny to park in front of his newly rented offices on Mulberry Street. As he pulled out of the car wash, seventy-five-year-old Frieda Feeny clipped Lawyer Calhoun's new car, taking off the driver's side door. The pompous barrister was, as could be expected, fit to be tied. He ranted and raved so loudly at the terrified Feeny woman, that Connie Crenshaw at the Toadsuck Florist called the city marshal.

When the marshal arrived, Lawyer Calhoun was screaming hysterically! "Oh quiet down, Mr. Calhoun. You lawyers are so materialistic—always focused on your possessions."

"How can you say such a thing?" asked the red-faced attorney, who hadn't stopped yelling at both poor Mrs. Feeny and Toadsuck's city marshal.

When Lawyer Calhoun finally stopped boiling and Mrs. Feeny had finally stopped bawling, after being publicly berated by the new lawyer, the town marshal made his point: "You have been so frantic about the damage to your new car that you haven't even noticed that your left arm is missing from the elbow down!"

"Oh my God," screamed Toadsuck's new attorney. "Where's my new gold watch?"

"Never Discuss Politics or Religion"

Clifton Pearson, Toadsuck's well-liked barber, who had plenty of opportunity to engage his customers in conversation, was once asked how he managed to keep so many friends despite their diverse opinions. Clif replied that from the first day he opened his "clip-joint," as the men in Toadsuck called it, he made it a practice of never discussing politics or religion. "You just can't win in either category," he pointed out. As an example he told about an incident that involved one of the town's sweetest natured women, Faustine Sweeny.

Faustine was a frequent passenger on the T&P train to Denison, where her sister lived. But as long as she had been riding the passenger train it still made her nervous. To calm her nervousness, Faustine took along her Bible and read it during the brief train ride. Clif said that the dear lady never tried to poke her religion down other people's throats, but she was a faithful believer.

One day as she started her regular journey to see her sister, Ruby Christine, the train had barely cleared the depot when Faustine took out her well-worn Bible and started to read. A man sitting across from her saw her reading and gave her a smile and a chuckle and went back to reading his newspaper.

A few minutes passed and he turned to her and said, "You don't really believe all that stuff in there, do you?"

"Of course I do," Faustine replied, "it's the Bible."

"Well what about that guy that was swallowed by the whale?"

"Oh, Jonah. Yes, I believe it, it's in the Bible."

The passenger asked, "Well how do you suppose he survived all that time in the whale?"

"I don't really know," replied the faithful Faustine. "When I get to Heaven I'll ask him."

"What if he isn't in Heaven?" the man asked sarcastically.

"Then you can ask him," Faustine answered.

Three Marbles

Back during the Great Depression, the folks in Toadsuck were hit just as bad economically as the city folks, who were more accustomed to an upscale lifestyle. I remember "Muddy" Rivers' produce stand by the side of the road just north of town. I tried to stop there anytime I was in the area as Muddy always had farm-fresh produce at a reasonable price. And he didn't have one of those fat thumbs that many merchants and butchers were famous for having to add a few ounces to the scales when their purchase was weighed. Although food and money were scarce at the time, Mr. Rivers' stand seemed to always be crowded. Not only because of the quality of his produce, but largely because the old practice of bartering was still in effect at Muddy's produce stand.

One day while buying a few pounds of new potatoes with their appetizing red skins, I noticed a small boy, delicate of bone and ragged, but clean, hungrily admiring a basket of freshly picked green peas. I couldn't help overhearing the conversation between Muddy and the boy.

"Hello Billy, how are you today?"

"H'lo, Mr. Rivers. Fine, thank you, just admiring them peas, sure look good."

"They are good, Billy. How's your ma?"

"Gittin' stronger alla time."

"Good, anything I can help you with?"

"No sir, just admiring them peas."

"Would you like to take some of them home?"

"No sir, got nothin' to pay for um with."

"Well, what do you got to trade me for some of them peas?"

"All I got is my prize Aggie, best taw around here."

"Is that right, let me see her."

"Here 'tis, she's a dandy, ain't she?"

"I can see that. Hmmmm, only thing she is blue, I sort of go for red! Do you have a red one like this at home?"

"Not 'zackley...but almost."

"Tell you what, take this sack of peas home with you and next trip this way let me look at that red taw."

"Thanks, Mr. Rivers. Sure will!"

Mrs. Rivers, who had been standing nearby, came over to help me. With a smile she said, "There are two other boys in Toadsuck like him. All three are in poor circumstances. The Depression has hit them mighty hard. Muddy just loves to bargain with them for peas, apples, tomatoes, or whatever. When they come back with their red marbles, and they always do, Muddy decides he doesn't like the red after all, and he sends them home with a bag of produce for a green marble or perhaps an orange one."

After listening to the exchange between Muddy Rivers and the boys and listening to his wife's explanation, I left the roadside produce stand smiling and impressed with this man known to all around Toadsuck as Muddy Rivers. A short time later I moved down to Dallas, but I never forgot the story of this man, the boys, and their bartering.

I returned to Toadsuck about a year later to visit friends. While I was there I learned that the incredible Muddy Rivers had just died, and they were having a family visitation that evening. My friend, knowing how I felt about the owner of the produce stand, asked me if I wanted to go with him to pay my respects. I agreed to accompany him to the funeral home.

We got in line to meet the family and say what few words of comfort we could offer. In front of us in line were three young men. One young man was in an army uniform, and the other two were neatly dressed in dark suits and ties. The three men walked to Mrs. Rivers, who stood smiling and composed by her husband's casket. One by one each of the young men gave Mrs. Rivers a hug and said a few words to her before moving on to Muddy Rivers' casket. Each paused briefly and gently placed his own warm hand over Muddy's pale, cold hand in the casket. Each then slowly turned and with glistening eyes slowly left the funeral home.

When I reached Mrs. Rivers, I reminded her who I was and how I remembered the story of the marbles. With moist eyes she took my hand and led me to Muddy Rivers' casket. "This is truly a coincidence," she whispered, "those young men who just left were the boys I told you about. They told me how they appreciated the things Muddy had 'traded' them. They said tonight Muddy couldn't change his mind about the color or size. They said they had come to pay their debt. We never had much of what the world calls wealth, but right now Muddy would consider himself the richest man in Toadsuck."

With these words, she gently lifted the lifeless fingers of her deceased husband. Resting underneath were three magnificently shiny red marbles.

Growing Old Gracefully?

Toadsuck's Silver Leaves Retirement Center made every effort to permit the town's elderly to "grow old gracefully." It was their practice to permit their residents to continue to live as normally as possible, although under twenty-four hour supervision by trained medical personnel. This policy included permitting each resident to bring his or her own automobile to the facility and drive it as needed, as long as they could maintain their Texas driver's license. This practice continued successfully for years without incident but was recently abandoned due to a frightening episode reported by one of the facility's residents.

The whistle-blower was eighty-three-year-old Mildred Puckett, mother of long-time Toadsuck resident Riley Puckett. Mildred, it seems, was invited out for a Sunday drive by Ina Lee Hopkins, one of Silver Leaves' earliest residents. Ina Lee was a familiar sight behind the wheel of her big 1938 Buick roadster. During the two ladies' outing, according to Mildred, "Ina Lee drove through a red signal light without so much as a pause to look for traffic crossing the main thoroughfare. When I saw this," Mildred said, "I thought I must be losing it, 'cause Ina Lee had never made such a driving blunder before. Then," continued Mildred, "a few blocks later, Ina Lee went right through another intersection when the light was red! Again, I thought my arteries were clogging up faster than I thought!

"For the first time since I've been riding with Ina Lee, I was getting nervous. So I decided to pay special attention to the next signal light to make sure I was seeing correctly. Sure enough, Ina Lee went through the next signal on a light as red as a beet! I thought it best for both of us if I would call this to her attention. I turned to Ina Lee and said, 'Ina Lee, darling, do you realize we

just ran three red lights in a row? You could have killed us!' Ina Lee, I'll swear, turned to me and said, 'Oh! I thought you were driving.'"

It was this incident that, to the disappointment of many residents, led to the revoking of resident driving privileges at Toadsuck's most prestigious retirement home.

Poor Choice of Words

Doctor Proctor, although he proved to be a good physician and became accepted even by Toadsuck's most contrary residents, was not without his share of events that caused him to waver in his initial decision to come to the area to replace the town's retiring doctor.

Most of these less than stimulating occurrences involved Toadsuck's infamous hecklers and domino parlor devotees like "Rusty" Samford, whose greatest contribution to Toadsuck was getting off the street when the town had a litter drive.

Rusty went to the doctor's office complaining of an undefined ailment. The doctor told him, "Mr. Samford, I can't find a cause for your complaint. Frankly, I think it's due to drinking."

"In that case," replied Rusty, "I think I'll come back when you are sober!"

It was patients like Rusty who made Dr. Proctor think less of Toadsuck than the community deserved.

The Dawn of Civilization

The fine folks who settled in the part of Grayson County that later became the Toadsuck townsite, while not ignorant, were not well acquainted with many of the more up-to-date niceties of the twentieth century. As an example, most homes in Toadsuck still had outhouses instead of flush toilets. One by one, as a sewer system was developed, the folks started tying on to the modern convenience. One of the last families to avail themselves of this newfangled way of life was the Duckworths.

Billy Earl and Justine had grown up having to go outside in all kinds of weather to answer nature's call. They now look back and laugh at the time their toilet paper had numbered pages. Justine told how one year for Billy Earl's birthday, Toad Richardson, in an effort to help nudge the Duckworths into modern times, went all the way to Denison to buy Billy Earl a suitable birthday gift. A friend of his, who had once lived in Fort Worth, put a bug in Toad's ear about a wonder he had seen at the hotel he had stayed in during an Elk's Club convention. The wonder was a hinged toilet seat that put comfort into the user's call of nature.

After locating the white wooden attachment for the commode, Toad neatly wrapped the gift in colored paper he saved from a gift they received for their last wedding anniversary. The result was a gift Billy Earl would long remember. It was remembered not only for its festive look, but largely because after carefully unwrapping it, Billy Earl, never having seen one, didn't know what the toilet seat was! He looked quizzically at Justine, who was just as confounded as her husband was. "Dunno, Dad," she said. She always called her husband Dad, as that is what the kids called him. "I'm sure the Richardsons meant well, but they should have spent their money on something more practical. What do you plan on doing with it?" she asked her bewildered husband.

"Been turning it over in my mind," said the recipient, "and maybe it's a lot more useful than we thought. After all, we're not so up to date on lots of things on the market. The tag on it says, 'Denison Hardware' so the city folks must be finding it useful or they wouldn't be carrying it in the store. My first thought is that the top part would make you a mighty fine dough board, and we could frame your maw's picture in the bottom part! Mighty thoughtful, I'd say, for Toad and Vera to give me a birthday present that the whole family can enjoy!"

"Once More, With Feeling!"

Although many of the tales I remember growing up in Toadsuck were humorous ones, some of the most enduring ones were those that left you with the feeling you had been hit in the gut by a medicine ball! One that falls in that category was a story told by Virgil Stamps, who had been hired by the Bethel Baptist Church in Toadsuck to be the church's choir director.

Virgil, ironically, hailed from Conway, Arkansas, which was only a stone's throw from Toadsuck's Arkansas namesake. This put him in good stead with the folks at Bethel from the get-go. One evening at choir practice Virgil was not getting the response from the group that he was striving for. He is said to have chided them for making melody without any feeling. "It is important to use your diaphragm when singing," he said. "But," he added, "feeling and understanding the words, is a must if you are to use your voice in praising God! When you don't sing from the heart it shows in the final product. If we truly want to please God with our singing, we must understand and feel the words the composer felt when he penned them. Most of us," he continued, "go through life mouthing lyrics to a tune we have heard all our church lives without truly understanding how their meaning effects our Christian walk!"

As an example, Virgil told about a fellow who died and was waiting at the Pearly Gates to be interviewed for admittance. St. Peter told him, "Before you can enter Heaven you must answer some questions."

"Let's get on with the questions, I feel I'm prepared for eternity."

St. Peter then asked the candidate, "Who were the first two people created on earth?"

"Adam and Eve," shot back the man without hesitation.

"Correct," said the gate custodian. "Now," asked St Peter, "What is the name of our Lord and Savior?"

To this the man answered, "Andy."

A shocked Saint Peter glared at the man in disbelief. "I've been guarding these gates for eons," said the saint, "and I've never had anyone give that answer. What makes you think the name of our Lord and Savior is Andy?"

Again, with full confidence, the man said, "Because we sang about him nearly every Sunday in church.... 'Andy walks with me, Andy talks with me, Andy tells me I am his own.'"

Splitting the Sheets

If there ever was a "perfect marriage" in Toadsuck, it was not that of Quinton and Mavis Bodine. Folks could hardly fail to know that Mavis had one heavy cross to bear, that of Quinton's less than moderate drinking. Friday night out with the boys was a regular occurrence every Wednesday, Thursday, and Friday, too! For some reason Quinton could hardly stand being at home after dark. Someone ventured that "Perhaps Quinton was afraid of the light?"

As he was always a good provider and a good daddy to the Bodine's three kids, Mavis just couldn't bring herself to quit Quinton. After all there had never been a divorce in Mavis' family. Of course no one in Mavis' family had ever been married to Quinton Bodine! In a leap of desperation, Mavis went to their pastor, Brother L. C. Tremble. It was Brother Tremble who had, in happier times, tied the knot for Mavis and Quinton.

Pastor Tremble gave Mavis some advice that would, inadvertently, lead the couple in the exact direction Mavis wanted so to avoid—divorce! Well meaning as it was, the good pastor's homespun marriage counseling backfired on the Bodines and the reverend, too. He suggested that scaring "Demon Rum's hold on Quinton" out of the woman's otherwise acceptable husband just might be the best approach.

"And, Pastor," asked a desperate and open minded Mavis, "just how can I do this?" The preacher advised that on a night she was sure Quinton would come home "soused," she should drape herself in a sheet and hide behind one of the two juniper bushes that bordered the couple's front walk.

"When Quinton starts into the walkway, jump out and holler, 'I'm the devil, and if you don't stop drinking, you're going straight to hell.' This," said Brother Tremble, "ought to shock Quinton into his senses."

Mavis wasn't long in waiting for her chance to put Pastor Tremble's advice into practice. Friday afternoon Quinton called Mavis from the job saying he and a couple of the guys from the feed store where he worked were going to visit his foreman in the hospital. This was, Mavis knew, an excuse for Quinton to come home late. After she had supper and read the paper she got one of her best bed sheets, draped it loosely over her head, and took up a position behind the evergreen bush as advised.

She lurked there about two hours before she saw Quinton staggering up the road in a condition that left him unable to hit the ground with his hat. As he neared the couple's house she drew herself up to full height and recited her lines to herself over and over. Then came the dramatic, magical moment that, she hoped, would save her marriage and Quinton from a life of a sot! Mavis, at just the right time, jumped out from behind the juniper and in a loud shrill voice shouted, "Boo, I'm the devil!"

Before she could finish with the rest of her warning, Quinton stuck out his right hand and in a slurred voice said, "Shake hands, we're related, I married your sister!" And the fight was on. During the ensuing marital spat, Mavis split her perfectly good bed sheet.

Mavis made history that night in Toadsuck. No, Quinton wasn't scared out of his drinking habit, but Mavis set the stage for becoming the first one in her family to get a divorce.

Even Dogs Got Feelings!

Clinton Culpepper just couldn't resist the sign in the window of Toadsuck's Main Street Café. "Homemade beef stew" was Clint's culinary weakness. After taking a chair at the table nearest the kitchen of the café, he asked Maudie Mae Grubbs, the café's long-time noon waitress to bring him a big bowl of the tempting stew.

The day's special lived up to the expectation that had set Clint's mouth to salivating. Maudie Mae had seen to it that Horace Clowers, the café's daytime cook had filled the biggest bowl in the kitchen, you know the type—the ones used to give kids a haircut—to the brim with the steaming stew. Clint hardly had time to give a silent prayer of thanks before he attacked the concoction with a big soup spoon. His Nettie Sue had never produced a mouth-watering stew like Horace Clowers could make. "If only I'd married Horace," he laughingly muttered between bites of the steaming stew.

Far too soon his bowl was empty, and Clint was rummaging in his pocket looking for a generous tip for Maudie Mae. Clint placed a quarter under his bowl so that Maudie Mae would be sure to see it when she cleared the table.

As Clinton paid his tab, Wilfred Clowers, who was Horace's brother and manager of the Main Street Café, asked him if everything was okay. "Nothing finer than Horace's beef stew, especially on a cold day like today," replied Clint. "Only complaint I have is that I was uncomfortable the whole time I was eating Horace's stew. Your dog sat in the corner and stared at me during my entire meal!"

"Easy to explain," replied Wilfred, "you was eating out of his favorite bowl."

"Suffer the Little Children to Come Unto Me"

Perhaps some folks might criticize me for writing so much about the children of Toadsuck, however, my fondest memories of growing up in the small Grayson County town involve the children I grew up with. I remain impressed with the lessons taught by these innocent, down-to-earth children of a less complicated time. Children in their innocence had a way of breathing life into those principles that to the adults of Toadsuck was an expected way of life.

One example of this was Lou Ann Snively, the daughter of Homer and Ardenia Snively who moved to Toadsuck from north of the Red River. At an early age the Snivelys had given Lou Ann chores to do that would develop her self-confidence. They gave her jobs normally reserved for those older than she. Jobs they knew she could succeed at.

Her strong soprano voice could be heard ringing from the children's choir where she learned to stand before the congregation and sing without the normal childish shyness evident in children of her tender age. It was no surprise that she was selected to play a lead part in her first grade production of *Heidi*. But her crowning glory seemed always to shine in Miss Ellinor Benidict's fifth grade art class. I sat behind Lou Ann that year and was not surprised that "Miss Ellinor," as we called her, permitted Lou Ann to work without the close supervision that those of us less mature were given.

Lou Ann's self-confidence was made abundantly clear one morning just before the school let out for the Easter holidays. Miss Ellinor, as usual, was walking around in her classroom looking over the shoulders of her pupils and offering criticism as needed. She came to Lou Ann, who was hunched over her drawing board busily at work on the day's assignment, "a suitable Easter theme."

"And," queried Miss Ellinor, "what are you drawing, Lou Ann?"

Without hesitation, Lou Ann blurted out for all to hear, "I'm drawing a picture of God!"

"But," interrupted Miss Ellinor, "no one knows what God looks like."

"They will in a few minutes," replied Lou Ann in a respectful, but assertive tone of voice. It was at that moment I learned the real meaning of confidence from a ten-year-old.

Trial and Error, or, Even God Learns From Experience!

Little five-year-old Callie Dunsmore was visiting her grandfather, who operated the Toadsuck Hardware and Stove Repair store, when she made a profound discovery that her grandmother thought worth repeating.

Little Callie was sitting across the table at dinner one evening when she noticed the reflection of her grandpa in the mirror of the buffet. She looked carefully at his time- and weatherworn hands. The hands of the old man were brown and spotted. She looked down at her youthful hands and made a mental comparison. She then looked at her grandfather's wrinkled, weather-beaten, face topped by a shock of snow-white hair. She paused a moment before glancing in the mirror at the fair skin of her own childish face. Then, as though she had gained enough evidence to present a credible case, Callie looked her grandpa squarely in the eyes and asked, "Grandpa, did God make you?"

"Sure he did, Callie."

"Well, then," she added, "did God make me?"

Without even a pause, her grandfather assured the child, "Certainly God made you!"

"Well, Grandpa," responded the little girl, "don't you think he does better work now than he used to?"

The Night Santa Claus was Seen in Toadsuck, Texas

The tiny town of Toadsuck is not far enough north of Dallas to be anywhere near the fabled North Pole, but it was far enough that it got considerably more snow than we were accustomed to seeing or driving in. I remember one Christmas when my sister, Nell, and I were still children and were not yet callous enough not to believe in Santa Claus.

Although our house was already festively attired for Christmas, and the cotton batting under our tree was laden, as much as our meager income would permit, with the presents for each of our four family members, it was decided that we would spend Christmas with our grandparents, who lived just north of Toadsuck. By the time we packed our old model car and mother had put in a couple of her homemade quilts, "Just in case of car trouble on the road," our first snow of the season was coming down in big wet flakes. It was already sticking on most surfaces.

"You know," remarked my cautious father, "the roads north of here will be axle-deep by now. Get in the car, Flossie," he hurried my mother as she returned from her trip inside the house, to be sure the lights and stove were off, which was a regular ritual before every trip anywhere. My sister and I awaited our departure in the backseat of the old Chevrolet. We fondled our few wrapped gifts, still trying to guess the contents of each of the tinsel-decorated packages. This was not to be one of our longer journeys, as Grayson County was only a couple of hours' drive from our house. Void of any problems, we should arrive in time for supper, as we called dinner then. That is if our hosts waited for us, as they surely would.

We had only been on the road about an hour and a half when Dad made the startling announcement. "Flossie, it's just too dangerous to drive all the way tonight!" The snow on the old highway toward Denison was deep in the wet, sticky snow. One could not see the shoulder of the road or the dangers that lay beyond. The windshield wipers had long since given up on fighting to keep the windshield free of the blanket of snow that covered the glass every few minutes. Nell and I, in our childish minds, only thought of the wonderful snowman and snow ice cream the fluffy precipitation would make. The dangers of driving on the slick surface were adult worries.

Dad finally decided, with Mother's concurrence, to stop in Toadsuck and spend the night with one of Dad's cousins and get a fresh start in the morning. Although not expecting us, "Aunt Dee," as we called her, welcomed us with open arms. That is the rural way of life. As was the practice in those days, the adults took the beds and we kids were bedded down on the floor on pallets made from Aunt Dee's snugly quilts. She even gave Nell and me two of her prized feather pillows. We insisted on keeping our Christmas gifts in the room where we slept. After all, Christmas was only a day away, and we wanted to make sure Santa Claus didn't have to hunt for these advance presents from our family.

One thing Nell and I had already noticed upon arrival was the huge rock chimney over the family's fireplace. Just perfect for a Christmas delivery, we thought. That is, if Santa knew where Toadsuck, Texas, was. Little did we know!

Nell had, after the drive north, drifted off into a deep, comfortable sleep. I, being curious about being in a strange place, was still wide awake. Then it happened! I remember that long-ago Christmas with its startling apparition like it was yesterday. A scratching noise drew my attention to the room's only window. The rural night was the blackest I'd ever seen. Then I saw it, or was I dreaming, I wondered. Plain as day, peering in from the darkness was Santa Claus. His fur-trimmed red suit and hat were as bright against the pitch-black night as they were in the seasonal Coca Cola advertisements! I rubbed my sleepy eyes with a mixture of childish fear and disbelief. Here in the rural community of Toadsuck, Texas, was the most dreamed of figure in a child's life!

I eased my hand across the quilt covering my sleeping sister. I didn't want to frighten her, but here was a sight I didn't want her to miss. And, she could verify I wasn't dreaming, a confirmation I was in dire need of. I remember feeling for the Christmas gifts we had brought, to be sure they wouldn't get left behind.

With great trepidation the next morning at breakfast, I told the adults what I had seen, or thought I had seen. I had prepared myself to swallow the hoorawing adults generally give kids who in their naiveté fall for a bogus story or situation. I told my parents and Aunt Dee what had happened the night before. Instead of an embarrassing amount of ridicule, Aunt Dee, with a sly laugh, confirmed that we had, indeed, seen the jolly old elf, in person.

"Don't you know," said Dad's cousin, "old Santa seems to take pity on us folks who live in a town with such a funny name? I kinda think that because so many folks don't think there is such a place in Texas as Toadsuck, just like so many folks don't believe there is a Santa Claus, the old boy likes to show up here now and again just to prove folks wrong on both counts!"

I was perfectly satisfied with Aunt Dee's rationalization about Santa's nocturnal visit. As a former skeptic about both Toadsuck and Santa, I could see how showing himself from time to time, especially to citified folks like Nell and myself, would help his cause. And the word of mouth publicity it would generate for the little community of Toadsuck couldn't hurt anything, either.

The vivid image of the benevolent bearded man in the red suit stayed with me all during the holidays that year. It was some days after New Years that Dad, always honest with us kids, told us that Aunt Dee's son, Herbert, had been asked by the Toadsuck school to play Santa Claus in the school's Christmas play that year. He told us that Herbert, always one for a practical joke, had been rehearsing at the school when we arrived that snowy night. When he returned and found out about the Dallas visitors and that two little kids were sleeping in his room, he couldn't resist carrying his Santa role a little further!

Dad said that after Herbert had his laugh about Santa's visit, he neatly folded the school's costume and put it in a box in the closet where it would stay, prepared for Santa's next visit to the community of Toadsuck!

Who Says Texans Talk Funny?

The fact that we Texans are sometimes ridiculed for our regional accents may hurt but may, to our chagrin, be justified. The criticism is borne out by this story of what happened a few years ago in the little town of Toadsuck.

Joe Bob Dodds, the librarian at the Toadsuck lending library, suggested that the boys in Mr. Snodley's high school wood-working class build and install a nativity scene for the Christmas season. He said the added decoration in front of the town hall would draw the shoppers' attention to the real purpose of the holiday while they vigorously pursued the commercial side of the Christmas season. "It also would provide the woodworking class with some variety in their projects, instead of the usual construction of martin houses and magazine racks for the bathrooms," said Joe Bob. "The martin houses haven't attracted one family of birds in my yard in three years, and," he added, "many folks in Toadsuck have canceled their magazine subscriptions, claiming the editors were using 'words that were too big.'"

Mr. Snodley thought the project was a great idea. He said he believed he could get the local churches to donate much of the material, and he was sure his neighbor Newton Rumley would let them use his live jackass and a bale or two of hay to make the scene more realistic. The inspirational artwork was erected by the fifteenth of December. This coincided with the arrival of the visit of the national leader of the Knights of Columbus. The local lodge was delighted that this honored guest would be able to see the community's recognition of the season's origin.

The leader from Boston, Massachusetts, complimented the local lodge head for the town's decoration but said he had questions about the scene. "Why," he asked, "are the three wise men all wearing firemen's hats?"

"We have," retorted the Toadsuck lodge head, "tried to adhere strictly to the Bible's story of the birth of Christ. You obviously aren't familiar with the scriptures."

"I believe I am well versed in this particular story," argued the Bostonian.

"Well then, you will recall the scripture saying that the three wise men were coming from afar."

Long Ago in Toadsuck

No one is around who remembers Brady Tate, one of Toadsuck's very early residents. As a matter of fact, few still remember the old Toadsuck Saloon around which the town was founded. But stories still abound about the early days of Toadsuck and some of its more colorful residents. I guess with no one left to dispute them, it is pretty safe to repeat the stories that have been passed from one generation to another. Which brings up Brady Tate.

Brady, it is said, wore that low spot in the hardwood floor in front of the beer tap in the old Toadsuck Saloon. To hear folks tell it today, Brady pretty much occupied the exact same spot Saturday nights for most of his years until his liver gave out! The story most often related is about the night his drinking really did him in.

After drinking most of the night, "Baldy" Quince, the saloon's long-time barkeep, came to Brady and told him the saloon was fixin' to close. Brady tried to stand up straight to get ready to leave, and he promptly fell flat on his face. He was able to right himself with a little help from Joe Bob Jordan. He tried to stand again with the same results. Brady decided to crawl outside and hang out, in hopes the fresh air would help sober him up. Once  outside, he tried to stand up again, and again he fell on his face! As long as he was already down, Brady figured he would just crawl four blocks home. Once there, he again tried to stand up but fell flat on his face. Brady was, by this time, exhausted. He gave up and crawled to his bedroom, where he fell across the bed and was asleep before his throbbing head hit the pillow.

Brady awoke the next morning to find his wife standing over him shouting at him. "So, you've been out drinking again!"

"What makes you say that?" Brady asked with that innocent look on his battered face.

"Baldy at the saloon called; you left your wheelchair there, again!"

The Age of Innocence

Hardly anything their eight-year-old son, Timmy, did or said surprised Buddy and Joleen Pate. The precocious and imaginative little boy seemed always to be at the head of the class in Toadsuck.

But when little Timmy announced that he and his next-door playmate, Sally Conway, who was the same age, were going to get married, Buddy felt it was time to bring the adventurous kid down to earth. Joleen felt the same. After all, living in a fantasy world was not unexpected for kids Timmy's age, but these fantasies need to be reinforced with facts, Joleen thought. Timmy just couldn't be allowed to grow up taking matrimony so lightly, reasoned Joleen. After all, that's what she did, and she ended up with Buddy.

So being the vigilant mother she was, she asked Buddy to try to impress Timmy with the seriousness of marriage. As it turned out this was a father-son talk that was overdue! Buddy called little Timmy into the family's garage, where there was nothing to distract the boy. Sitting the lad in front of him on a workbench, he asked him, "Timmy, I hope you and Sally have thought this marriage thing out thoroughly."

"We have, Daddy," replied Timmy.

"Well just where are you and Sally going to live after you're married?" asked Buddy.

"We have decided that we will live part of the time at her house and part of the time at my house," replied Timmy, confidently.

"And," continued his father, with Joleen's instructions breathing down his neck, "just what are you going to do for money?"

"We have both agreed to pool our allowances," answered the eight-year-old.

Buddy hesitated a bit and stammered some as he broached the next question. "Normally, son, after marriage children come along. Have you and Sally thought about that?"

"Sure have, Dad," said the boy confidently. "We both agree that when Sally lays her first egg, I'll step on it!"

This couple, thought Buddy, are better prepared for marriage than most couples in Toadsuck.

The Fast Thinker From Toadsuck

One of Toadsuck's best minds was a long haul truck driver whose parents were financially well fixed enough to send him to school in Denison. Ol' Billy Bob was Toadsuck's pride and joy in the higher education department. Few, if any, could outthink that ol' boy when it came to the trials and tribulations of everyday living! No doubt about it! The family's investment in ol' Billy Bob's education had paid off. That is probably why he got the job at Toadsuck Nationwide Freight Company. There warn't no flies on Billy Bob when it came to good ol' common sense thinking. Folks in the Toadsuck Barbershop still tell the story of how Billy Bob handled himself when he got stuck under the Katy railroad bridge just north of Denison in the summer of '64.

There's a "low bridge" sign about a quarter mile west of the bridge, and the bridge is plainly marked 13 feet 6 inches. However, one has to admit, the numbers have become faded by time. But most folks who drive up there know the Katy has the lowest bridge in North Texas! Ol' Billy Bob must have been dozin' a little when he sailed under that bridge pulling TNF's standard 14-foot trailer. And, Whomp!, there he was, stuck tighter than a wood tick on a redbone hound! Pretty soon ol' Billy Bob had traffic backed up for two miles. This, as could be expected, caused plenty of ill feelings among North Texas drivers, not to mention serving to attract the Texas Highway Patrol stationed between Denison and Toadsuck!

Sure enough, in his rearview mirror, Toadsuck's pride and joy saw the recognizable two-toned car slowly making its way past the string of irate drivers stalled behind him. One could almost hear the wheels in ol' Billy Bob's head whirring as he began to put his higher education to work for him. Billy Bob watched as

the approaching black and white car's buggy-whip antenna stopped whipping back and forth, and the red-faced patrolman, ticket book in hand, approached his side of the truck.

"Stuck, are you?" asked the patrolman with a dangerous smile on his face. Then Toadsuck's educated long haul driver really made his family proud of their investment.

"Naw," said Billy Bob, with a choirboy's expression, "I was delivering this here bridge when I ran outta gas!"

Fort Worth, Where the Streets are Paved With Gold

The community of Toadsuck, friendly as it was, was lacking one thing for those who were ambitious. It offered little in the way of a future. Like other small, rural towns of its day, Toadsuck lost many of its residents to the larger, bustling cities where their growth made jobs more plentiful to those willing to work. The less adventurous advanced in small steps like moving to nearby Denison, where they could still be near their family and friends. Others ventured out to the real "bright lights" cities like Fort Worth.

Such was the case of the Sweeny twins, Willard and Dillard. The strains of "Pomp and Ceremony" had hardly died away following their graduation ceremony at Toadsuck High School until the boys were talking about fleeing the family bonds and seeking their future in Fort Worth. They had already saved enough to buy a one-way ticket on the T&P to that city, where they were sure they could improve their station in life. "After all," they said in unison, "any place progressive enough not to take its name after a saloon must be on the doorsteps of the future.

A move into such a beehive of activity created apprehension in the hearts of both boys, confident as they were. But, they thought, hadn't the class president said "The world is there for the taking, and we, having withstood the rigors of living in a place called Toadsuck, are up to the challenge?" With this deeply motivating spirit driving them on, the Sweeny twins found themselves boarding the four-thirty special to Fort Worth. Look out city, here we come, they thought. Perhaps the fact that an aunt living in the city had offered them temporary quarters in her home dulled their anxiety somewhat.

At any rate, they had said their goodbyes in Toadsuck and the die was cast! The events surrounding their arrival in the bustling city known for its stockyards and high flying cowboys put to rest any apprehensions about making a living "Where the West begins." They had hardly walked a quarter mile away from the T&P depot when they spotted a ten-dollar bill laying on the sidewalk. "Look, said Dillard, there's a ten-dollar bill, let's pick it up!"

"No!" said Willard, emphatically, "Let's not work on our first day here!"

Even Vets Need Good Bedside Manner

Folks in Toadsuck considered Ol' Doc Bixby the best veterinarian in all of North Texas. His dedication to the practice of animal medicine was evident not only by his success rate, but in the way he tried to help bring qualified persons into the profession. He had a standing arrangement with the College of Veterinary Medicine at College Station, Texas, that each summer they would send a senior to intern with him. Although these "vet pups," as he laughingly called them, were paid very little, the practical experience they received under his tutelage was more than adequate compensation for their labor.

Doc Bixby's practice was largely farm and ranch animals, but he had his share of house pets as customers, too! An incident that occurred in the summer of 1916 almost cost the good doctor a customer of long standing. Had the incident not had a comical side, the good doctor might have come down on his young charge like a ton of bricks. But, as is the case in most adversities, there was an up side. The incident serves to vividly point out that even veterinarians need to develop a positive bedside manner. Not for their patient, as is the case with regular people doctors, but for the owners of their patients, who often feel that their animal is like one of the family.

Such was the case in point: this year's intern, a twenty-two-year-old from Houston. His summer was about over when Dr. Bixby called the young Aggie into his office one morning.

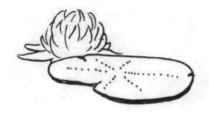

"Got an emergency for you to start your day. One of our long-time, well-to-do clients has a pet parakeet that is suffering from cross-beak. A common malady among the colorful, feathered, pets. The bird has been in the family for nearly twenty years. The lady is most distraught. I want you to get over there as soon as you can and get this customer satisfied."

"But," interrupted the intern, "I have never seen or treated a cross-beak. Do you think I am ready to tackle this emergency?"

"Listen closely to my instructions, my boy," said the kindly doctor, "and you will handle this case like a pro." Dr. Bixby then slowly laid out the procedure for the nervous student. "Take these little clippers with you and snip off the end of one of the bird's beaks. This will enable you to force the beaks past each other, which will allow the bird to return to his normal eating habits."

"Is there any unexpected thing that I should know about and be prepared for?" inquired the student, not wanting to be caught unprepared in front of the good customer.

"Only one thing," replied the doctor, impressed with the young man's forethought. "After snipping the end off the bird's beak, there may be some slight bleeding. In this event, you will find in your bag a thin wire with an electrical plug. This is a 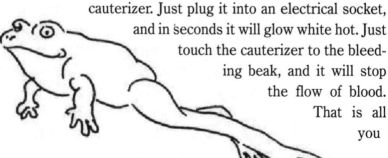cauterizer. Just plug it into an electrical socket, and in seconds it will glow white hot. Just touch the cauterizer to the bleed-ing beak, and it will stop the flow of blood. That is all you need to know about this procedure. I am sure you can handle this emergency, so be on your way. Remember this customer is counting on you to bring her pet back to normal living." With this vote of confidence from Dr. Bixby, the student grabbed his treatment bag and sped away.

Upon arrival at the client's residence, the student rang the doorbell, which was soon answered by a matronly woman, who, by her clothes, seemed to be very affluent. When the student identified himself, the now smiling woman cheerfully invited him in. "Please help my precious Bobby bird," gushed the woman in an emotion-choked voice. "He's been in the family over twenty years, and he's like one of my kids."

The student observed the distraught pet owner nervously watch his every move as she continued to gush forth with superlatives describing the bird. When the student took the clippers out of his bag, the lady looked at the sharp instrument and asked, "Is this going o hurt my poor Bobby? Can you give Bobby bird something to keep him from feeling pain?"

Wanting the customer to be happy, the student, not knowing if the procedure was painful or not, took out a small vial of ether and moistened a cotton swab enough to place it over the parakeet's face. The bird almost immediately fell asleep. This pleased the doting woman very much. "Thank you, my boy, for being so considerate," she said.

The young man set to work clipping the end of the bird's top

 bill off just slightly. This permitted him to uncross his bills and eat normally once again. However, just as his mentor had said, the student noticed a small drop

of blood oozing from the tip of Bobby bird's clipped beak.

Momentarily forgetting that ether is a most explosive chemical and that the bird's little lungs were full of the stuff, the student, feeling pretty proud of himself on this his first emergency call alone, remembered the cauterizer Doc Bixby had tutored him about. He plugged in the instrument, and seconds later the wire glowed white hot. He perched the family pet on one finger and held him in the air where he could better see. He then lifted the cauterizer and touched lightly to the parakeet's beak. To the surprised of both the student and the matronly client, with a muffled WHOOMF!!, the parakeet exploded!

The room was filled with an atmosphere of shock and gloom! The room was also filled with Bobby bird's mortal remains in the form of small pastel green and blue feathers that swirled about the room and floated lightly to the hardwood floor. Realizing that his unprofessional conduct might have damaged the veterinarian's relationship with the client, the student looked straight into the client's still glazed-over eyes and in a consoling voice said what he thought would be a gesture designed to repair any breach he might have created. "Of course, Ma'am, there will be no charge!"

Adding Insult to Injury

No one ever claimed that the *Toadsuck Sentinel* would ever win an award for its coverage of the local news, nor would its writers ever win the Pulitzer prize. But being the only newspaper in the small Texas town made it worth more than just a lining for the bottom of a bird cage. Caroline Harris, the paper's editor, had, over the years, endured her share of criticism for the emptiness of the little weekly rag. But, despite its heartaches, the

paper not only provided a living, but it gave her
a certain stature in the meager society of
Toadsuck. She was always invited to the
important social events in the town.
Events like the monthly meeting of
the community's volunteer fire
department, the Toadsuck Women's
Garden Club meetings, and, above all,
the meeting of the town council at the
town hall. All in hopes of receiving free newspaper coverage of
their special interests.

Despite all of these free "mashed potato and English pea" luncheons and dinners Caroline attended, the newspaper, even with its all-important obituary column and a detailed report on all marriages and anniversaries in the county, was hardly a cornucopia of news.

Caroline was brought to a state of nervous prostration one week when, due to a gut-wrenching hangover, "Pink" Brasher, one of the staff's best typesetters, spilled the entire week's obituary column and had to reset the movable type, which resulted in several of the obituaries being out of place. The typesetter tried to smooth things over by adding a line at the end of the column that read, "The *Sentinel* deeply regrets the disarray of this week's obituary column, but it is through no fault of the paper. Those included in this week's column unfortunately did not die in alphabetical order."

It was just such an edition as this that caused some folks to say, "You can read the *Sentinel* and eat cotton candy, and when you are through you won't have anything on your mind or stomach either!"

Patriotism is Only Hide Deep

While the folks in Toadsuck grew up mighty proud of their country, especially Texas, World War II proved that for some, one's patriotism could only be stretched so far! This is borne out by personal conversations Lonnie Ray Carson had with his friends in Toadsuck after his return from Europe following a four-year hitch in the army.

While Newt and Betty Lou had brought up Lonnie Ray to be as flag-waving as the next guy, they didn't do their teaching under constant fire from a bunch of "furriners" hell bent on killing Lonnie Ray! His European combat time had taken its toll on the Grayson County boy. First of all, Lonnie Ray had little say-so in his decision to demonstrate his love of country! A select group of his neighbors made that decision for him.

One day, shortly after he graduated from Toadsuck High School, Lonnie Ray, who seldom got any mail at all except for a letter or two from the famous Charles Atlas Body Building Company, got an official-looking letter from the Grayson County Draft Board. The letter informed him that, "Being in Class A, your friends and neighbors have selected you to represent them by serving in the United States Army."

What an honor, he thought, as he proudly refolded the letter to show to his parents. Both Newt and Betty Lou had kept up with the war through the Denison newspaper and by listening to Gabriel Heater on their Philco radio. They knew the dangers that their unsuspecting son would face in either theater of the war. Nevertheless he was given a small "stiff-upper-lip" pep talk by his father and a hug and kiss by Betty Lou as they put him on the Texas and Pacific train to Denison, where he was to report for his physical exam, which none of the three had any doubts he would pass. (After all he had built himself into quite a muscular young man without the expense of the Charles Atlas course he once considered after reading of it in a comic book.) But that was when the Carson boy was a "ninety-eight pound weakling!" It only took three summers working at Denmon's Redy-Mix Concrete to envelope Lonnie Ray's skeleton in muscles he never thought he would see in his mirror. Now he was off on the first step to prove his manliness—the passing of his physical.

He had barely been declared physically fit for duty, when he found himself in full olive drab in Camp Quonset, Louisiana. His letters home, while reflecting a bit of the normal homesickness, still expressed his appreciation that his "friends and neighbors" felt confident enough in him to ask him to represent them in this global conflict. This patriotic attitude was to set the tone of Lonnie's letters back home until he reached his overseas assignment. It was there, in the muddy foxholes of far-off Belgium, that the tenor of his letters started to show wavering on his part.

The loss of comrades, several of which were also selected by their Toadsuck "friends and neighbors" to represent them in the bloody war, took its toll on Lonnie Ray's enthusiasm for defending his country! Not that the cream of Toadsuck's youth had lost his patriotism. As he later, upon returning home, told friends, "Staying alive soon loomed high on my list of priorities!"

A conversation Lonnie Ray had with Clif Pearson in Clif's barbershop summed up Lonnie Ray's feelings about his wartime service pretty well. He told the friendly barber, "Last time I was in class A when the war started. Next time I'm gonna do my darndest to be in class 'B': B here when they go, and B here when they come back!"

He Sleeps Well When the Wind Blows

A rancher who owned a small spread between the Grayson County town of Collinsville and the nearby community of Toadsuck was in need of a ranch hand. He put out the word at the Toadsuck Feed and Hardware store as the town had no newspaper, and most menfolk could generally be found at this establishment at one time of the day or another, most any day of the week. This was partially due to the almost marathon domino game that was in progress when the store doors were open. Those who didn't actively participate stood around and hoorawed the losers and hoped the winners would be kind enough to buy a round of soft drinks from the "Coke box" in the back of the store.

Bob Turpin, who had inherited the popular store from his father, sent over a robust young man to apply for the ranch hand job. Unemployment in Toadsuck was almost an unheard of thing, and the civic-minded store owner didn't want to see the statistics shoot up because this young man was out of a job. He arrived at the ranch just as the rancher finished loading his pickup with feed for the cattle in the pasture.

The rancher asked the young man what ranches he had worked at. The well-built, rather slow talking applicant said, "I have never worked on a ranch, but I sleep well when the wind blows at night!"

The rancher, while not pleased at the man's lack of experience, was more puzzled at his unusual answer. "Well," continued the rancher, "do you have any reference from places where you have worked?"

"No," replied the young man, "but I sleep well when the wind blows at night!"

Again, the sturdy young man's reference to his sleep habits puzzled the rancher. Maybe the young man, while physically fit for the demanding job, is slightly retarded, wondered the rancher to himself. After all, he was not well known in Toadsuck and had no work history in that part of the county. The rancher, who was desperate for some help, told his ranch foreman to give the man a job on a trial basis. "We should be able to determine in a month's time if he is up to the task."

The foreman showed the new hand where he would sleep in a small room in the barn that had been a tack room. A few nights after the young man had been hired, there arose a howling blue norther so typical of the North Texas prairie. "Go wake up the new man, and have him bring the ponies in from the corral to the barn. Have him hang up the harnesses and other tack in the tack room. Be sure he puts plenty of hay in the horse stalls, as we may be in for a long siege of bad weather."

The foreman went to the makeshift room where the new ranch hand slept. He called loudly but got no response from the young man. The foreman rapped forcefully on the door but heard no evidence the new man was responding. Out of desperation, he lunged against the door, which yielded to the force. Once inside he found the new man sound asleep, apparently unaware of the storm. In a fit of disgust, the ranch foreman left the room with its snoring ranch hand and returned to the barn to commence doing the tasks requested by the rancher.

When he checked the corral, he found the young ponies had already been brought to safety inside the barn. All tack had been neatly hung in its proper place in the tack room. A check of the stalls revealed they had been supplied with fresh hay and water. It was then, and only then, that the rancher and his foreman realized what the young man was trying to tell them when he said, "I sleep well when the wind blows at night!" It's too bad, thought the rancher, that we can't all say, "I sleep well when the wind blows at night."

"I Will Make You Fishers of Men"

For weeks, little eight-year-old Maudie Frickert had been looking forward to a Saturday fishing trip with her dad, Delbert. But when the day finally arrived, it was raining. Maudie wandered around the house all day grumbling as she peered out the windows. "Seems like the Lord would have known it was better for it to rain yesterday than today."

Delbert tried to explain how important the rain was for the farmers and gardeners of Toadsuck. But Maudie only replied, "It just isn't fair."

Around three o'clock the rain stopped. There was still time for the father and daughter to get to the river and fish. Maudie quickly loaded the fishing gear and they headed out. Because of the rainstorm, the fish were really biting. Within a couple of hours they returned with a full stringer of fish.

At the family's fish dinner that night, Maudie was asked

to say grace. She concluded by saying, "And, Lord, if I sounded kinda grumpy today, it was because I couldn't see far enough ahead."

Both Delbert and his wife, Floyce Jean, concurred later that evening that the Lord's selection of those appointed to teach us His will was not limited to adult men.

Other Books by the Author

A Treasury of Texas Humor

This delightfully funny book covers every facet of Texas humor from life on the range to church, politics, Texas women, history, and hysterics. *And* it's a book your kids can read.

1-55622-693-4 • $14.95 US
$23.95 CAN.
200 pages • 5½ x 8½ • paper

A Treasury of Texas Trivia

Discover a host of little-known facts about the history and people of Texas.

1-55622-693-4 • $14.95 US
$23.95 CAN.
200 pages • 5½ x 8½ • paper

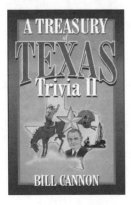

A Treasury of Texas Trivia II

A Treasury of Texas Trivia II continues the amusing, interesting, factual, and sometimes ridiculous bits of information begun in the first book.

1-55622-699-3 • $14.95 US
$23.95 CAN
224 pages • 5½ x 8½ • paper